HUNTING BIGFOOT

A TALE OF REVENGE

BY ERIC S BROWN

SEVEREDPRESS

HUNTING BIGFOOT

HUNTING BIGFOOT

Danny shivered, pulling his jacket tighter around him. The wind was intensely cold. Danny felt like he was freezing to death. He could see his breath in the frigid early morning air. The sun hadn't come up yet. Its early rays were just only now cresting the distant mountain tops through the trees. Danny blinked at them, his eyes still accustomed to the darkness. The night had been a long one. He, his brother, and his father were still on the hunt for the wolves that his dad thought were responsible for killing their cattle. And they'd lost more than a few in the last two weeks. His father thought it was the work of wolves because the corpses were always ripped open and fed upon, covered in deep claw slashes. Danny's father knew it was illegal to hunt wolves. They were protected animals. Something had to be done though and since the local authorities weren't doing anything, his father was taking matters into his own hands at this point.

The hoarse, strained voice of his father howled in the direction of the rising sun. Danny didn't know how the man was able to still howl at all.

He'd been doing it all night. None of them had ever hunted wolves before but his father told them that by howling he might get the wolves to howl back in response and then they would know where the animals were. . .at least to an extent.

Shoulders sagging in defeat as nothing answered him, Danny's father turned to look at him and Nathan. Danny did his best to keep his expression calm and determined, putting on a show of resolve for his father. Nathan, though, was done with trudging about the woods.

"Come on, Dad," Nathan urged. "This is pointless. We ain't never gonna find anything out here."

"You giving up on me, boy?" their father frowned as he eyed Nathan.

"I'm just telling you the truth, Dad," Nathan argued. "We been at this crap all night and haven't seen or even heard a darn blasted thing."

At first, Danny thought their dad was going to haul off and knock out some of Nathan's teeth for back talking him. The old man didn't though. His shoulders just sagged even more and he let out a sigh.

"Yeah, boy, I guess you're right," their dad admitted. "Let's get headed back home. I'm sure your mother is going crazy worrying about us."

Danny let a slight smile creep onto his lips. He wanted to hug Nathan for having the nerve to stand up and say what needed to be said. His older brother was one tough bastard, just like their father. The two of them often butted heads these days but Danny knew they loved each other.

Their father led the way on the long trek home. The sun continued to slowly rise. They didn't need flashlights anymore to find their way. Its dim rays were enough for them to see. Danny wished the sun would warm things up too but at this time of year, in the late fall, it wasn't a sure thing that the day would get warm at all. There was frost on the ground. Danny shivered again as another gust of wind whipped around him. None of them saw the thing coming until it was too late.

Their father heard something tearing through the woods towards them first. His head jerked around in the direction of the noise as the monster, there was no better word for it, came bursting out of the trees. It was on top of the old man before he could even raise the barrel of his rifle. Claws gleamed in the early light as they flashed through the air. Blood splattered as most of the right side of the old man's cheek was torn away. A hair-covered fist followed blinding speed, plunging into and through the center of the old man's body.

"Dad!" Nathan yelled as Danny stood, frozen, watching it all happen in utter shock.

The beast stood over eight feet tall, yellow eyes burning with feral rage. It was covered head to toe in filthy, brown hair. The thickness and strength of its muscles were clear even through the hair covering them. The beast pulled its clenched fist free of the old man's body, allowing Danny's father to topple to the ground as Nathan's shotgun thundered.

The sound of the blast made Danny flinch and in the process woke him up from the stupor he was in. Danny heard himself screaming as the slug Nathan fired found its target. The hair-covered beast that had just killed their father staggered backwards but didn't fall. Somehow the thing stayed on its feet despite taking a near point blank hit from a 12 gauge. Danny heard Nathan working the weapon's pump to chamber another round. The beast roared and lunged forward, making a grab at Nathan. His older brother tried to dive out of the beast's path but it was too fast. Over-sized, human-like hands caught hold of Nathan by his shoulder and yanked with impossible power. Nathan's body tore apart down its center below his neck in an explosion of blood that flew everywhere.

Danny felt wet, warm droplets splash onto his face. His stomach churned as his heart pounded so hard against his rib cage Danny thought it might burst. Mouth dry and hands shaking, he jerked the .30-.06 his father had made him carry up to his shoulder and fired at the beast. The high caliber round ripped a red gash across the beast's left cheek. Working the bolt of the rifle with a speed born of adrenaline and fear, Danny fired again. This time his shot pierced the beast's right shoulder leaving a gaping exit wound in its wake. He expected the beast to charge him like it had his father and Nathan but instead, blood running down along the front of his body from its wounds, the beast turned tail, sprinting away into the trees. Danny managed to get off a third shot before the thing was completely out of sight but had no idea if it made contact or not. Then as suddenly as it had appeared, the beast was gone. Danny was alone in the woods.

Running to where his father lay, Danny dropped to his knees. "Dad? Dad?" he pleaded on the verge of tears, hoping against hope that his father was still somehow alive. The beast's fist had gone through the old man just below his ribs.

"Da. . .Da. .Danny," his father sputtered, coughing red spittle as he tried to speak. "I. . I'm sorry."

"Dad, hold on," Danny begged, tears now rolling down his cheeks and body shaking with sobs. "I'll get help."

"You. . .get out of here, boy," his father told Danny and then left this world for the next one. His eyes rolled up to show only whites.

"Dad?" Danny gently shook his father. "Dad,

please don't die, don't leave me alone."

Danny's father lay still and his body limp. He was gone and Danny couldn't do a blasted thing about it. Getting to his feet, Danny snatched up his .30-.06 and worked its bolt to chamber a round. With a grim expression of determination on his face, he marched into the woods. Danny searched and searched for hours before exhaustion claimed him. Unable to go on, Danny collapsed, passing out. He thudded onto the ground, unconscious.

Something slapped against his face. Danny moaned, opening his eyes. A man in a deputy uniform was leaning over him.

"Wake up, kid," the man's gruff voice barked.

"Wha. . .Where am I?" Danny stammered.

"You're lucky to be alive, kid," a deeper voice called out from behind the deputy. It belonged to Sheriff Stanton. "You wanna tell us just what the hell happened out here?"

****

Danny woke up howling like a madman, hands clenching his sheets so hard that his knuckles were white. Drenched in sweat, Danny struggled to calm down and catch his breath as he saw the walls of the hotel room around him and not trees. Dim, pale light spilled in through the window from the streetlight outside. Trembling, Danny threw back the sheets and sat up on the side of the bed. The soles of his bare feet thudded onto the cool carpet of the floor. It took everything he had to keep from vomiting. The shrink Danny had been seeing for the last few months thought it was all P.T.S.D. from his time in the Middle East. Danny had never told her the truth. His childhood had taught him the hard way that no one believed in monsters. . .not even when the evidence was there staring them right in the face.

Running the fingers of his right hand through his wet hair, Danny looked over towards the room's window. He took a deep breath and sighed. He knew the nightmares were never going to end until he found the bastard thing that had killed his family and sent it to Hell. But that was why he was here, wasn't it? To find the creature and make it pay. The years Danny spent in the service taught him how to kill and now it was time to put those skills to use in a manner that mattered to him on a personal level and not just for some distant idea, no matter how important that idea might be.

Danny headed for the shower. Stripping off his sleep shorts, he stepped into it, letting warm water flow over him. Closing his eyes, he leaned into the spray. Nothing truly brought him peace though. After cleaning up, Danny dried off and got dressed. It was still quite some time until the day began for most people in the small town of Clinton, North

Carolina. The place hadn't changed much in all the years Danny had been away. It was almost surreal to be back. Main Street was just how he remembered it as Danny drove into town. Even the diner where his mother and father took him every Sunday after church was still open and in business. Chuck, the diner's owner, surely had to have passed on by now, but one of his kids must have taken it over and kept it going.

Thinking of Chuck's Diner made Danny think of his mother. He missed her so much. She'd died while he was in his first year of service. Danny hadn't come home for her funeral. He hadn't been at a point mentally where he could then. The town of Clinton held too many bad memories for him. It took a long time to come to terms as best he could with all that crap and figure out how to deal with it. What was his plan to deal with it? Vengeance, plain and simple. Danny knew that was his only hope of ever having a normal life. To that end, he had not only finally returned to Clinton but called in all the favors owed to him. A killer he might be but the thing Danny planned to go up against was one too and this area was its home turf. Danny knew that going out into the woods after the beast alone was pretty much suicide even for someone as skilled in death as he had become. That was why Danny called in the favors, to get the help he needed. His buddies should be arriving later today and then he could get started on setting things right.

Shrugging on a shoulder holster, Danny filled it with a Glock 20. He then pulled on a jacket to conceal the weapon and left his hotel room. The air outside was brisk. Spring was ending but the full heat of a southern summer hadn't begun yet. Danny lit up a cigarette, taking a long, deep drag from it. He exhaled the smoke slowly, savoring its flavor. Smoking was a bad habit and Danny knew it but there was no way in hell he could live without it until things were settled between him and the beast that was out there in the woods. The nicotine helped to settle his nerves. His stomach rumbled, demanding breakfast. Danny started down the street to see if Chuck's was open yet. There were a few fast food joints in Clinton that he knew would be open at such an early hour but his childhood memories of Chuck's drew him towards it. The diner was close enough to walk to from his hotel.

The streets were barren and lit solely by streetlights. Danny finished his cigarette and tossed it onto the pavement, grinding it out with his right boot before continuing on. A car came down the road, headlights burning through the dark of the early morning. It slowed and came to a stop just ahead of where Danny stood. He walked up and over to the car's passenger door as the driver rolled down its window.

"Danny?" the woman in the driver's seat asked. "Is that really you?"

Eyes going wide, Danny realized who he was talking to.

"Hannah?" he stammered.

Smirking and shaking her head, Hannah asked, "You headed to Chuck's?"

"Yeah. Yeah I am," Danny nodded, recovering from his surprise at bumping into her.

"Hop in then," Hannah told him.

Danny slid into the car's passenger seat, unable to take his eyes off of Hannah. She barely seemed to have changed at all despite the years that had gone by. Just as beautiful as ever, red hair spilling over her shoulders, her green eyes met his. Danny's heart skipped a beat. Hannah hadn't lost her ability to make him feel butterflies either. They'd dated briefly in high school before Danny went into the service but things just hadn't worked out. Danny was just too messed up back then to really give Hannah what she needed. . . and she wasn't willing to basically becoming a nurse to another kid with P.T.S.D. and a ton of emotional baggage. Tearing his eyes away, Danny looked out of the window.

"So. . . what brings you back to Clinton?" Hannah asked. "Honestly, I didn't think you would ever be back."

"Business," Danny answered as they pulled into the lot outside Chuck's Diner. He got out of the car, starting for the diner's door.

"Whoa," Hannah called, getting out after him. "After all these years, that's all I get? Not even a 'hey can I buy you a coffee?'"

Danny knew that he shouldn't give into how he was feeling, that he needed to stay focused, but frag it, she was his weakness.

Frowning, he turned to face her. "Hannah, I. . ."

"You're still just as messed up as you ever were, huh?" Hannah chuckled though they both knew she was only half joking.

Danny managed a grin. "Yeah. I guess I am."

"Fine," Hannah smiled. "I'll pay for your coffee then. Come on."

She walked by him, heading on into the diner. Sighing, Danny followed after her.

Chuck's Diner had just opened. A waitress Danny recognized as Chuck's daughter, Michelle, greeted them.

"Well I'll be gosh darned," Michelle lit up. "Danny Taylor, as I live and breathe, I didn't think I'd ever be seeing you around here again."

"I've been getting that a lot this morning," Danny answered, giving Hannah a wink.

"Here," Michelle ushered the two of them into a booth. "You just tell me what you want. Jake'll have it ready in just a few minutes."

"Thanks," Hannah nodded. "I think I'll just have a coffee."

"Me too," Danny chimed in.

"You sure?" Michelle pressed them.

"We're sure," Hannah smiled. "Thank you, Michelle."

Michelle placed a hand on Danny's shoulder and gave it a gentle squeeze. "It really is good to see you again, Danny."

Leaving to fetch their coffees and take the order of another couple who had just come in, Michelle scampered away.

"Well?" Hannah leaned forward in her seat.

"Thank you for the coffee," Danny answered, knowing she was waiting for more.

"Come on now, Danny," Hannah laughed. "I want to know what business you have here in Clinton. I mean really? This place is as small and backwards as it ever was."

"If that's true then how come you've never left it?" Danny countered.

"Clinton is my home," Hannah shrugged.

"I get that," Danny grunted.

"No you don't," Hannah argued. "You never did. All you ever wanted was to get as far from here as you could."

"Can you blame me?" Danny countered.

Hannah sighed. "No. . .I guess I can't, given everything that happened."

"Mom did everything she could to make things seem normal for me after. . ." Danny paused, his voice cracking. "After. . ."

"I know." Hannah reached across the table top to place a hand onto the top of his arm.

Danny pulled his arm away from her, his expression going dark.

"Look, Hannah," he told her, "I won't be in Clinton long, just a few days with some friends of mine who are on their way."

"Some friends, huh? And I guess they're part of this business you have to take care of," Hannah stared at him.

Michelle came bouncing back, their coffees in her hands.

"Here ya go," she said placing them onto the table.

Sensing the tension between him and Hannah, Michelle frowned. "You sure you guys don't want something to eat?"

"We're fine, Michelle," Danny said, more gruffly than he intended.

"Okay then," Michelle, clearly hurt by his tone, left them alone again without another word.

"Danny. . ." Hannah started.

He cut her off. "You don't need to be worried about me, Hannah. Really, I'm the best I've been in a very long time."

"You don't seem it, Danny," Hannah countered. "You seem the same as ever."

Her words stung him but Danny tried not to let it show. He took a sip of his coffee.

"Danny, why are you here? Really?" Hannah pressed.

Looking at his watch, Danny placed his coffee back on the table and got up. Reaching for his wallet, he tossed a twenty onto the table.

"I've got somewhere to be but it was nice to see you again, Hannah," Danny told her.

"Hey, wait," Hannah called out as Danny turned his back on her, heading for the door.

This time Danny found the strength to resist her. He left the diner and kept going down the street.

****

The Ford Mustang roared along the two lane road, shifting gears and gaining speed. Jarvis was smiling like a fiendish devil in the driver's seat. In the passenger seat, Derrick was holding on for dear life.

"Fragging hell, man!" Pete yelled from the backseat. "Take it easy!"

Next to Pete, Ron had his eyes closed and was snoring.

"Relax, man," Jarvis laughed. "I got this."

"Yeah, well, you're going to have a floorboard covered in vomit too if you don't cool it," Pete warned.

Jarvis slowed the car with a scowl on his face. "You puke back there and you'll be cleaning it up, A hole."

The sun was coming on. Jarvis adjusted the visor above him to block the bulk of its early rays from his eyes. He'd been driving all night and the short burst of speed had been more to get his adrenaline pumping to keep him awake than just showing off. It was fun though. Jarvis couldn't deny that. Any chance to mess with Pete always was.

"I can't believe we're really doing this," Derrick said, relaxing and releasing his death grip on the dash.

"What?" Jarvis quipped. "You ain't into monster slaying?"

"There's no such thing as monsters," Ron's cold, hard voice said from the backseat.

Jarvis looked at the big man via the rearview, wondering if he'd really been asleep at all.

"All that matters is that the captain needs us," Derrick said.

"Derrick's right," Jarvis agreed. "The man saved all our butts more times than I care to remember."

Though he sounded reluctant, Pete chimed in, "We have to be there for him, no matter what. He'd be there for any of us and you know it."

"This place he's got us going to sure is way the hell out in the middle of nowhere," Jarvis commented.

"It's where he grew up," Derrick said. "Don't you remember him talking about it?"

"No, I fragging don't," Ron growled.

"How much longer until we get there?" Pete asked, eager to be out of the backseat and away from Ron.

"About ten minutes according to the GPS." Jarvis dug around to get out a cigarette. He shoved it between his lips but didn't light up. "Did the Cap say anything about this monster we're going after to you guys? All he told me was that it lived in the woods out here and killed his family when he was a kid."

"For what I gather, it's supposed to be a Bigfoot," Derrick smirked.

"No fraggin' way," Pete almost sounded excited. "That's messed up, man."

Ron looked over at Pete. "Don't tell me you believe in that crap."

"There's a ton of evidence to support something like a Sasquatch existing," Pete grinned. "I mean, really, all the sightings, the footprints, videos like the Patterson footage. They're these giant, ape-like creatures who. . ."

"Pete," Jarvis interrupted. "I think we've all watched enough TV to get the gist of what a

Bigfoot is, okay?"

Derrick gave Jarvis a silent look of thanks for shutting Pete up.

"I still say there ain't nothing in the woods we're headed for except the Captain's bad memories and nightmares," Ron huffed.

"And if you're wrong?" Pete challenged him.

"We've brought along enough gear to blow whatever is out there to hell," Ron answered. "Ain't nothing on this Earth that can't be killed. Just a matter of how much it can take before it goes down."

****

Sheriff Levy Stanton wrinkled his nose at the stench coming off the corpses sprawled out on the ground. There were two of them, a man and a woman. From the look of things, they had come up into the mountains for a romantic camping excursion only to get torn apart. Their tent was in shreds, dried blood was everywhere, on the ground and the trunks of the trees surrounding the clearing where they died. The man was opened up, his red slicked, purple intestines spilling out of him like decaying snakes. His eyes were wide, forever locked in an expression of sheer terror. The woman was worse though. Both of her legs were ripped completely from her body and missing. She was naked from the waist down which made the sight of her even more sickening. The damage done to her wasn't all below the waist though. There were gashes on her cheeks and neck as if some wild animal with huge paws had clawed at her. Levy raised a hand to cover his mouth, feeling sick. It was far from the first time in his career that he'd been around dead bodies but these two. . .there was something about the savage way they were mutilated that was just beyond inhuman.

Clinton was a small town and as such didn't have as much crime as the large cities. That was part of what made Levy opt to take over for his father, the previous Sheriff Stanton, instead of taking a better paying job in law enforcement elsewhere. Murder wasn't unheard of but it was rare. Levy couldn't explain why his mind leapt to the conclusion that what happened to these two poor bastards might be murder instead of just another animal attack.

One of the first things Levy noticed after arriving on the scene were the strange footprints throughout the camp. They were deeper than a man should be able to make and odd in that the giant feet that made them were bare. Levy couldn't explain them either. He was well aware of the local legends of ape-like creatures up in these mountains. Those stories had been around since he was a kid and far longer. His father had dealt with the most famous case involving the supposed monsters when the Harkin family was murdered. The father of the family and his two kids had come up here hunting for something that was preying on their cattle but only the youngest of them had come home. The dad and older brother were said to have been killed by the beasts. That was what the surviving kid swore. Levy's father had closed the case calling the whole thing nothing more than a tragic bear attack. The kid never gave up trying to tell folks otherwise though and eventually ended up the local loony bin. Levy had read the case files and remembered the pictures of footprints almost identical to the ones he was seeing now within them. In the official report though there was no mention of them or why they were even included in the case's paperwork. With a shake of his head, Levy chased the insane thoughts that were going through his mind away.

Two of his deputies, Chad and Warren, were getting ready to help the EMTs bag up the corpses for transport into town. His head deputy, Brook, walked over to him.

"You okay, sir?" she asked, concern in her voice.

Levy nodded. "As good as can be expected, I reckon. Not everyday we have to deal with crap like this."

"We found both of their IDs," Brook told him.

"Brent and Becca Hyatt from over in Waynesville."

Levy shook his head sadly. "Nobody deserves to die like this."

"No, sir, they don't," Brook agreed. "We likely never would have found them but the woman was able to get out a call to 911 somehow before. . .well, you know."

"She did?" Levy asked, surprised as most of the time there wasn't any signal in these mountains. Even on a clear day under the best circumstances getting a call out was nothing short of a minor miracle.

"Guess she got lucky. . .just not lucky enough for it to matter," Brook commented and then went on, "According to the dispatcher, they had to trace the signal. At first they thought it might be a prank call because she wasn't able to tell them anything about what was happening or where she was. They say she was just screaming."

"That would make sense," Levy grunted. "So, what's your take on this mess?"

"An animal attack, sir," Brook gestured at the mangled corpses being shoved into the body bags. "Had to be."

Brook stared at him for a second. "Wait, are you thinking it's something else?"

Levy wasn't about to give voice to the thoughts that were going through his head. They were just too crazy. He countered instead with another question, "How do you explain the footprints then? Hillbilly cannibals?"

Snorting, Brook smirked at him. "Really, sir? I think you've been watching too many horror flicks."

"Brook," Levy pressed her, "I'm serious. How do you explain them?"

After a moment, Brook answered, "I can't but. . ."

Levy waved a hand, dismissing the whole conversation. "Get some molds taken of them. It'll be better to have them than not just in case and make sure they get sent out to someone who can tell us what leaves prints like that."

"Yes, sir," Brook frowned, clearly still thinking about the prints now too.

"I'm headed back to town. I'll be at Chuck's grabbing a late breakfast if you need me. You got this from here?" Levy asked.

Brook nodded.

Levy started to walk back through the trees towards the trail that led down to where his patrol car was parked but stopped, turning to say, "Oh and Brook. . ."

She looked at him expectantly. "Yeah?"

"Keep all this out of the damn news," Levy ordered. "Make sure none of our boys or those EMTs say anything to anyone. Folks'll raise all hell if this gets out before we know more about what happened."

****

Danny stood in the parking lot outside of the hotel he was staying in. Ron, Pete, Derrick, and Jarvis pulled into the lot, their car zooming into a parking space close to where Danny was standing. The quartet jumped out of the car, slamming its doors.

"Hey, man!" Pete beamed.

"What's up, Captain?" Jarvis smiled.

"Sir," Ron gave a sharp nod of his head.

But it was Derrick who reached him first, extending a hand. "It's good to see you, Danny."

He took Derrick's hand, shaking it. Danny looked them all over.

"I'm so glad all of you came," Danny said sincerely. "Come on," he ushered them towards his room. "We've got a lot of work ahead of us."

Danny had drinks, ashtrays, and seats ready for the guys. Ron snatched up a beer, twisting off the bottle's cap, and plopped into a chair. Jarvis lit up a smoke but remained near the room's door as the others all sat down with Ron except for Danny.

"So you wanna tell us what we're really doing here, sir?" Ron rumbled, taking a chug of beer.

Danny stared at Ron. "I wasn't messing with you guys, Ron. What I told you was the truth."

"Wow," Pete grabbed a beer of his own. "That's freaking awesome."

"I guess that means we're really going monster hunting, huh?" Jarvis asked.

Danny nodded. "That we are."

"Captain," Derrick said, "We brought everything you asked us to."

"Good," Danny nodded. "We're going to need all of it."

"It's a hell of a lot of firepower," Pete laughed. "This monster of yours really that tough?"

"Hell, is it even real, sir?" Ron glared at Danny.

"Hey!" Derrick shouted, springing to Danny's defense. Ron stood up, facing him.

"Whoa," Danny moved between the two of them. "Settle down."

"It's a valid question," Ron pointed out. "A lot of guys come home utterly screwed up, Captain, and you know it."

"My monster isn't just in my head, Ron," Danny assured the big man. "I wish it were but it's not. The thing is very, very real. It killed my father and brother when I was a kid and killed a lot more people since then too. I plan on making the bastard thing pay. That's why we're all here. Someone has to stop it and the local authorities won't even fully admit that it's real, much less go after it."

"I read up on what I could about this area," Pete

spoke up. "He ain't kidding. There have been dozens upon dozens of missing person cases that have been unsolved and a ton of animal attacks too that left people torn up so badly some of them still haven't been properly identified."

"Ron, if you want out, I get it," Danny told the big man. "I'm not your commanding officer anymore and this isn't the Sandbox. I can't order you around. All I did was ask for help."

"I ain't meaning no disrespect, Captain," Ron shrugged. "It's just. . ."

"A lot to take in and accept," Danny admitted, "But I promise you, I am not making any of this up. The monster I asked you here to kill is real and if we don't stop it. . ."

"Who will?" Derrick finished for him. "We're here. We've got the skill and the weapons. It's up to us to get this done."

Ron nodded and sat back down, reaching for a second beer, having already finished his first.

"It's too late for us to head into the woods today," Danny told them all. "And we're not about to go in blind after this thing at night. So enjoy yourselves, boys, and get some rest. We'll gear up and roll out at first light."

There was plenty of fast food on the table with the beers and ashtrays too. Derrick, Pete, and Ron tore into it, munching on burgers, cheese steaks sandwiches, and more.

Jarvis gave a slight nod of his head, letting Danny know that he wanted to talk outside, alone. Danny followed him outside, lighting up a cigarette of his own. The two of them stood there smoking.

"It doesn't take a psych degree to see that you're wound pretty tight, sir," Jarvis commented. "You sure you got this?"

"I got this," Danny promised. "I've waited most of my life for this, Jarvis."

"Yeah," Jarvis nodded, "That's pretty clear too."

"Look, what do you want me to say?" Danny challenged his friend. "Do I have tunnel vision where that thing out in the woods is concerned? Hell yeah I do. Am I scared of the thing? Only a fragging idiot wouldn't be. But does this need to be done? Yeah. Yeah it does and for more than just my family. You heard Pete in there. That thing is still out there killing even all these years later. It's got to be stopped and we're the people to do it."

Jarvis grunted and exhaled the drag he'd just taken from his cigarette. "I'm just saying you need to be aware of how wound up about this you are. Maybe let one of us take the lead out there."

"Really?" Danny eyed Jarvis. "And just who would you put in charge, Jarvis? You?"

"Hell no," Jarvis shook his head.

"Then who? Ron doesn't even really want to

be here. He's trying not to show it in there but Pete is scared to death of what's coming. And Derrick, well. . ."

"You're not giving Derrick enough credit," Jarvis argued. "He's gotten himself a lot more together than he was back in active service days, sir."

"That so?" Danny scoffed.

"Yeah, it is," Jarvis answered firmly.

Danny frowned. "You really don't think I can handle this?"

"I didn't say that, sir," Jarvis corrected him. "Not exactly. I am just suggesting that it might be a good idea for you to be the guiding hand but let him be the one making the hard calls."

Danny thought about what Jarvis was saying for a second. Maybe Jarvis was right. . . to an extent.

"Okay," Danny agreed. "If Derrick is up for it, so I am."

"Fair enough," Jarvis smiled. "We should likely get back in there before all the food's gone, eh?"

"Go on," Danny gestured at the door. "I'll catch up in a minute."

Jarvis disappeared back inside the hotel room. Danny took a drag from his cigarette. It was almost time. Tomorrow, everything was finally going to be okay again when the creature out there in the woods was dead and sent back to whatever hell gave it birth.

****

Hannah twisted and rolled in her bed, restless and unable to stop thinking about Danny. She'd gone to bed early with the intent of getting a bit of extra sleep. Tomorrow was a big day. A corporate group out of Asheville had hired her to take them up into the mountains for a team building exercise. It was the best paying gig Hannah had landed in a while. Her "guide" business survived mostly off the tourists who came up to see the leaves in the area during Autumn and she was careful enough with her money to make that work. As excited about the job as Hannah was, that wasn't what was keeping her awake.

The last thing she'd expected today was to run into Danny Harkin. It didn't help that he was just as hot as ever with his rugged body and sad expressions. She hated herself for caring about him but the truth was. . . Hannah hadn't ever really gotten over Danny.

In high school, they were inseparable. They were both misfits. She was the girl who loved the woods so much that no one else could understand Hannah's passion for it. She spent a great deal of her time camping. While Danny was the nut job. That's how everyone thought of him back then. He'd been a normal kid like everyone else until his father and brother were killed. After that, despite the best efforts of his mother, Danny had been in and out of mental institutions for years. Then his mother had started drinking right around the time that Danny finally seemed to be getting himself together. She went from his caretaker to a burden that was holding him back almost overnight.

The two of them had met at school. They'd been in the same history class during their sophomore year. For Hannah, it was pretty much love at first sight. She approached Danny and soon they were study partners. It didn't take long for them to be much more than that. Hearing Danny's story, one would have thought there was no way he'd ever set foot in the woods again. . . but that wasn't the case at all. Danny was constantly in the woods. Hannah hadn't understood why until later on in their relationship. He didn't love the woods like she did. Danny wasn't there to find peace or center himself. He was there in the hope of finding the creature that had killed his father and brother. It was, she found out, an all-consuming obsession. Danny was determined to find the monster and prove it was real.

His bedroom was like something from a crime movie where detectives were trying to figure out who a killer was. There were newspaper clippings going back decades pasted to his walls. At their center were several about the death of his father and brother. Hannah had talked with Danny about it all numerous times, doing all she could to get him to let his tragic past go and start living for the future. He was odd and messed up but so was she in her own ways.

The two of them dated all through high school until senior year. It was then that she finally broke up with him and he joined the military, shipping out before graduation. Having done everything she could to help Danny put the past behind him, Hannah just couldn't take his obsession anymore. Danny, too, seemed to be done with her, growing more and more distant, sinking into himself. The night of the prom, Hannah went to the dance alone while Danny was flying out to God only knew where with the unit he had been assigned to.

Hannah rolled onto her back, staring up at the ceiling. With a heavy sigh, she wondered if getting over Danny was even a possibility. In the years since their break up and Danny leaving Clinton, Hannah had dated a few guys. The most serious of them was Phillip. A good guy to his core, Phillip had pursued her for months before Hannah finally agreed to go out with him. From there, they took things slow, Phillip always doing his best to make her feel special. Their relationship was nearly the polar opposite of what she had with Danny. Phillip loved her and put

Hannah's needs first in every aspect of their lives but despite everything Hannah just didn't love him. No matter how hard she tried, those feelings just wouldn't come. Phillip began to sense how she felt after the first year and wasn't surprised when Hannah ended things between the two of them.

Reaching up to run the fingers of her left hand through her hair, Hannah lay there, wishing she could sleep. Every time she closed her eyes, Danny's face was there. Not the face from her distant memories but the face she'd just seen, grown up and rugged Danny who somehow had even darker eyes. Hannah knew that trying to restart things between them was likely the worst idea she could possibly have but nonetheless couldn't stop thinking about it. She hated herself for still having feelings for Danny, still wanting him after all these years.

If he was telling the truth, Danny wouldn't be in Clinton for long. After she finished up with guiding her latest group through the woods tomorrow, Hannah promised herself that she would try to catch up with Danny one more time before he left. She had to if for nothing else than closure's sake.

****

It was still dark as the van bounced up along the gravel road leading into the mountains that surrounded Clinton. Jarvis hated the piece of crap, missing his Mustang that they'd left behind at the hotel. Somehow it was him who always ended up driving. He blamed that on the Sandbox. Jarvis was the squad's driver then, too.

The road they were on didn't go all the way but then there wasn't one that did. Jarvis slowed the van and brought it to a stop just short of the dead end at the far side of the clearing ahead of them. Shoving the van into park, Jarvis turned to look at the others. Ron was already armed to the fragging teeth. The big guy cradled a pump action 12 gauge in his lap. Like some reject extra from a Rambo movie, Ron wore a bandoleer full of shells for the weapon. There was a Desert Eagle holstered on his hip and a large knife strapped to the side of his right boot. Pete sat next to Ron, holding an M4. Derrick was in the rear of the van with them, leaning against its side wall, clutching an M4 as well. Danny was up front with Jarvis, a Barrett M82 propped between his legs against his seat. All of them, himself included, wore camo fatigues meant to blend into the woods that they were headed for.

"You ready for this?" Jarvis asked.

"You bet your fragging arse I am," Danny answered, grim and serious.

The five men exited the van. Jarvis locked it with the remote on the keys and then shoved them into his pocket.

"Looks like we got some company," Pete commented, nodding his head towards another van that was parked in the clearing.

Danny hadn't noticed until that moment. The predawn shadows were deep and thick at the edges of the clearing. He saw it now though. The other van had the words *Davis Tours* painted on its side. The sight of those words froze Danny in place. It had to belong to Hannah. He'd heard that she'd become a sort of tour guide in these mountains during his time in the service.

"Something wrong, Captain?" Derrick asked, walking up to him.

"No," Danny lied. "We'll just have to watch out and make sure whoever these people are, they don't become collateral damage."

"Yes, sir," Derrick agreed. "You heard the man, boys. Remember to check your targets when we're out there."

"Roger that," Jarvis and Pete chorused in unison while Ron only grunted his acknowledgment of what had been said.

"Alright, Captain," Derrick said, "This is your show. We've got your back."

Danny took a compass out from his pocket. Its needle went nuts. He'd expected as much but had to see if things were still the same up here after all the years that had gone by. Something in these mountains messed with electronics on a level he didn't understand or really care to. He'd heard folks talk about some sort of geological formation or abnormal amount of iron deposits in the area. Whatever it was, the effect messed with cell phones and radios too. Once you were up high enough, one could basically forget about any communication with the rest of the world that was tech based.

"Well that's weird," Pete said, looking at the compass.

"Nah," Danny shook his head. "It's really not."

"But. . ." Pete started.

"Let it go, Pete," Derrick ordered and Danny was thankful that he had. Danny didn't feel like trying to give Pete a science lesson in something he didn't fully understand himself.

"Can we get on it already?" Ron huffed. "We're losing daylight."

Jarvis laughed at that. The sun was just beginning to rise.

None of them truly had tracking skills but Danny had spent years roaming these mountains. Danny wasn't worried however. He could feel it in his bones that they weren't going to need to find the beast. His gut told him that the thing would find them, given time.

Danny took point as they started up the trail, out of the clearing, that led into the woods. Derrick was right behind him, keeping close. Then came Pete and Jarvis while Ron brought up the rear. The five men fell into a brisk but cautious pace as the sun rose over the mountain tops.

The day got hot quick as the squad marched on, deeper and deeper into the woods. The cover of the trees didn't help too much with the sun. These woods weren't as dense as some and were spotted with numerous small clearings throughout.

It was close to noon before Danny decided they all needed a break.

"Let's take five," Danny barked. Derrick nodded his approval. Jarvis had convinced Danny to let Derrick take the overall lead while they were out here.

Jarvis leaned against a tree, lighting up a cigarette. Pete took a seat on the ground, tearing into a power bar with a ravenous hunger. Ron stood in the center of the clearing they were in, eyes scanning the trees all around them. Derrick chugged down half a bottle of water before screwing its cap back on. Danny let them all do their own things. His mind was on the beast that was out here somewhere. The thing was in his nightmares almost every night but Danny hadn't seen it in real life since the night it took his family from him. He'd always wondered how something so large could manage to hide out here undetected. It just didn't seem possible but obviously it was.

In all his time as a kid searching for the creature, Danny never found anything that could be used to prove its existence. He wasn't here to find proof so that he could get help against the creature now though. Those days were long gone. Today, the fragging thing was going to die and he was going to be the one to kill it.

****

Not a freaking thing was going right about Hannah's day so far. She'd gotten up late, was exhausted from her lack of sleep, and the dang van had nearly broken down on the way up the mountain. . . and now she had this crap to deal with.

"Yeah, we lied about that," Martin smirked at her.

It took everything in her to keep Hannah from breaking the kid's jaw. Right off, she saw something wasn't right about the "corporate group" that hired her and now Hannah was finding out why.

"We didn't lie about the money though!" Rachel piped up.

Hannah's head jerked around to glare at the redhead.

"Really," Rachel assured her, shrugging off her backpack and producing an envelope out of it. Hannah could see it was stuffed with cash. "Here.

Take it."

"Whoa now," Jason stepped over to take the envelope from Rachel. "Let's not get ahead of ourselves here."

The fourth member of their group, Alex, kept his mouth shut, staying out of it all.

"So just who the hell are you people?" Hannah demanded.

"We're from Edgar University," Jason told her.

"You're students?" Hannah's cheeks were flushed with rage.

"Film students," Rachel confirmed.

"And where the hell did you get the money. . ." Hannah started.

"We didn't need a lot of gear for this shoot," Martin was outright grinning now, "so we had plenty left over from the grant we got to hire you."

"Come again? Just what the hell. . ." Hannah stopped, realizing exactly why the kids were up here and hired her.

Jason nodded. "That's right. We're hunting for the monster."

"You're crazy," Hannah met Jason's eyes. "I've been coming into these woods my whole life and never ran into anything out of the ordinary up here."

"You chose those words pretty carefully, didn't you?" Alex said, finally joining in. "Just because you've never seen the beast doesn't mean it's not real."

"Look, lady," Martin said, "We're paying you, aren't we? Shouldn't that be all that matters?"

"I don't need your money," Hannah snarled at the punk arse, blonde kid.

"Ms. Davis," Alex's voice was calm. "We were afraid you wouldn't take us on if you knew who we were and what we were doing right off."

"We're sorry about lying," Rachel pleaded, "We really are but we need to do this. Someone has to find the monster and prove it's real."

Hannah shook her head in disgust. "You kids don't know what the hell you're talking about. A lot of people, older and more experienced than you lot, have tried to find proof of the monster up here and failed."

"Sure," Jason admitted. "We know that and aren't denying it."

"Then what makes you think you can find it?" Hannah pressed.

"Whether or not we succeed doesn't really matter, Ms. Davis," Alex explained, "But we all need to do this and try."

"Yeah, this shoot means a lot," Rachel added. "It's our first and we need it to be amazing."

"Wait," Hannah was a bit confused. "Are you kids monster hunters or filmmakers?"

"A bit of both today," Alex told her.

Hannah sighed, shoulders slumping in defeat.

The truth was, though she'd never let the kids see it, she did need their money. Hannah had been counting on this gig to get the van fixed up and out of debt before the slow season set in.

"Okay," Hannah said.

"Okay?" Martin blurted out. "Does that mean you'll take us on up into the mountains?"

"I will," Hannah answered. "But there are going to be rules or we can end this little expedition right here and now."

"Let's hear these rules," Jason said.

"If we run into any kind of trouble, you do exactly what I say, when I say it, with no arguing or back talk," Hannah told them. "And no video of me. That's non-negotiable. Shoot whatever the hell else you want but not me. Got it?"

"Is that it?" Rachel asked.

Hannah thought for a second and then nodded, "I'll let you know if something else comes up but for now, sure."

"I would say those terms are more than agreeable," Alex smiled. "Thank you, Ms. Davis."

"Now that we've got all this crap settled," Martin spoke up again, "can we get on with it already?"

All of the kids were looking at her as Hannah sighed again.

"Come on then," she huffed, taking the lead. "Follow me. We'll head north and see what we run into."

The day was hot and stuffy as they trudged along. To Hannah's surprise, not a single one of the kids complained about it. They were apparently really all in on this expedition and determined to make one hell of a documentary out of it. Now that who they were wasn't a secret anymore, at least one, if not two of them, had a camera out at all times, filming everything they could. Hannah figured the universe was having a good laugh at her expense. After all the times she'd come up here as a teenager with Danny hunting for the monster, here she was again as an adult getting paid to do it all over again.

Despite everything, Hannah couldn't keep herself from liking most of the kids. Their resolve and maturity impressed her. Alex and Rachel came across as utterly sincere and good people. Jason was a bit of an ass but that just seemed to be his personality. He was focused and all business. She'd known plenty of entitled brats like him in her life and could endure putting up with him for a few days for the amount they were paying her. Martin was the only one that worried her. He wasn't like the others much at all and seemed to be just a snot nosed, immature punk who was mostly just along for the ride.

Stories about the monster up here had died down a bit now-a-days. Folks like these kids weren't nearly as common as they used to be. People still came looking but a lot less than back in the monster's heyday. Hannah wondered what got these kids interested in the Clinton monster anyway. Edgar University was a hell of a long way from the small town. Hannah knew they weren't going to find the monster. No one who went looking for the thing ever had. If these kids wanted to pay for the effort though, she'd take their money and not feel bad about it.

****

Sheriff Levy Stanton sat in Chuck's Diner reading the report that Dr. Hall had sent him. He read the words on the screen of his phone again. "While unquestionably inflicted by claws and teeth, these wounds do not match up with those that would be delivered by any known animals indigenous to this region."

Levy's plate was empty except for a few scraps of eggs which had long grown cold. His coffee had remained hot because Michelle kept popping by to top it up. He had been at the table for quite a while. Levy's mind churned with thoughts he didn't want to be having. His father hadn't talked much about the supposed creature in the mountains that surrounded Clinton. Whenever Levy asked him, his father always avoided the subject. Levy wondered now just exactly why that was. As a kid, he figured it was just because of what happened with the Harkin family. That mess had never sat well with his father and certainly not the town either. It was a blemish on an otherwise decent career. Levy's father seemed haunted by it even to him as a kid. There was nothing that his father could have done differently though, at least not that Levy could see. The killings had come out of the blue. One night everything was fine when folks in Clinton went to bed, the next, the entire town was living in fear. Doors were suddenly being locked and the number of guys open carrying on the streets doubled. Voices were raised against his father until a posse of sorts was assembled and headed out into the woods to find the animal that had killed the Harkins. Of course, the animal was never found.

Rubbing at the stubble on his cheeks, Levy sat his phone down and took a sip of coffee. His brow furrowed in thought, a frown on his face, Levy knew that whatever had torn the Harkins apart back then was what he was up against now. The animal or creature, whatever it was, had returned to Clinton. There weren't a lot of choices in regards how to deal with it. He could go full tilt, tearing into the mountains, hunting the thing or just quietly write off the deaths of the campers from the night before as a simple bear or wolf attack and sweep it all under the rug. Levy was beginning to question just how many times his father had done exactly that.

"You okay, honey?" a smiling but concerned Michelle asked, seemingly appearing out of nowhere. She'd swept in to refill his coffee again and caught him completely off guard.

Levy had flinched in his seat at the sound of her voice. His cheeks were red with embarrassment from that. Clearing his throat, Levy threw on a fake smile.

"Rough week so far, Michelle," Levy said, and that much was true. "We had some trouble up in the woods yesterday."

"Bad trouble?" Michelle's eyes widened.

"Can't talk about anything yet," Levy told her, "But it's not good. Don't you fret about it though, Michelle. We've got everything under control."

"More coffee?" Michelle raised the pot she was carrying towards his cup.

Levy managed a laugh. "No thanks. I'm pretty sure I've had too much already."

Reaching into his pocket, Levy deposited a twenty on the table to cover his meal and her tip. "You have a good one, Michelle."

"You too, Sheriff. . .And you stay safe out there," Levy heard her say behind him as he headed for the door.

Levy got into his patrol car. He sat there a moment watching the people on the streets of

Clinton. At this time of day, they were busy with folks rushing about to get their errands for the day done or heading back to work from lunch. Levy knew almost every face that passed his car. It was his job to protect them all and keep them safe. Since he had taken office, the thing in the woods had been quiet and forgotten about until this morning. Levy couldn't pretend it wasn't out there anymore without lying to himself and the whole of Clinton too. It was time to do something about the creature once and for all. Levy reached for his car's radio.

"This is Sheriff Stanton," he barked. "I want all available deputies to meet me at the station house pronto."

With that, he threw the gearshift of his patrol car into reverse, backing out of the space in front of Chuck's Diner. Levy didn't turn on the siren, that wouldn't do anything but set off a panic, but he still broke the speed limit on his way to get to the station.

When he got there, Chad, Warren, and Dodson were waiting on him. Warren and Dodson were both nursing mugs of steaming hot coffee while Chad was chewing on a mouthful of tobacco.

"What's up, Sheriff?" Chad said, after spitting a load of brown spit in the white, Styrofoam cup he held.

"Where's Brook?" Levy looked around.

"In her office," Warren answered. "You need me to go get her?"

Levy nodded. "Yeah, do that."

"Something wrong, sir?" Dodson asked.

Levy grunted. "Nothing we can't handle."

Dodson returned with Brook trailing on his heels.

"Sheriff," Brook tipped her head at him.

"Any word back yet on those prints?" Levy looked at her expectantly.

Brook shook her head. "Not yet."

Frowning, Levy looked around at his deputies.

"Here's the deal," Levy said. "As you know there's something up in the mountains that's killing people. We're not going to let that stand, folks. I want all of you to gear up and get ready to roll out. Brook, get Larson on the phone. We're going to need her dogs. Chad, get on the horn to Henry. Let him know he's going to be holding down the fort here alone until we get back."

"You serious?" Chad gawked at Levy.

Everyone else could see that he was so Brook asked, "Is this really a good idea?"

"You got a better one?" Levy shot back. "I am not my father, Brook. We're going at that thing up there head on. It's got to be stopped and it's our job to do it."

"Stop what, Sheriff?" Warren asked.

Warren was new to the town and department.

As thus, he didn't have a clue about what Levy was talking about.

"Exactly," Brook said. "What? What is it we're going up there to stop, sir?"

Levy was surprised she'd even still called him sir. Clearly, Brook thought he'd lost it. He couldn't rightly blame her for it either.

Ignoring her question, Levy stared at her. "Get me those dogs, Brook. Now."

"Yes, sir," Brook huffed and stormed off.

"Man. . .," Chad snickered. "She's ticked."

"Stow that crap," Levy snapped. "And get moving."

As his deputies scattered, Levy stood there amazed that he'd had the balls to actually do what he'd just done. He was likely the first sheriff in the history of the small town to pretty much admit what was going on in the mountains around Clinton and set out to really do something about it.

****

"Found those other people," Jarvis informed as Danny leaned against the trunk of a tree. Ron, Derrick, and Pete were close by as well. The sun was past its zenith in the sky and would soon be setting.

"Where?" Danny asked.

"They're a bit ahead of us to the northeast," Jarvis told him. "Looks like they're getting ready to make camp for the night."

"What ya thinking, Captain?" Ron said, walking over to join the two of them.

Frowning, Danny wanted to light up a smoke but kept himself from reaching for one. It wouldn't be a good idea under the current circumstances. Doing so would give away their position for sure if the creature they were after was anywhere near by.

"Derrick?" Danny looked at his second in command, who'd taken the overall lead for the time being.

"Our plan wasn't so much to really go hunting this monster of yours but to let it come to us," Derrick said. "We can't go setting up the traps we planned with civilians close enough to wander into them."

"Exactly what I was thinking," Danny agreed.

"We can't just go up to those folks and tell them to get the hell out of the woods," Pete chimed in.

"No, we can't," Derrick sighed, looking frustrated.

"I'd say our choices in what we can do are pretty limited," Ron interjected. "I mean, we don't even know where they're headed up here."

"True," Derrick admitted.

"Our best bet is going to be to put as much distance between us and them as possible and then just keep an eye out to make sure they don't come near wherever we do set up," Danny said.

"We're already going to be looking out for that monster of yours," Ron grumbled, "Now we gotta watch out for a bunch of idiots too?"

"Nothing for it," Derrick shrugged. "Looks like that's just how it's gonna have to be."

"Okay then," Danny looked around at the others. "If they appear to be heading northeast, we'll go northwest and keep moving tonight."

"In the dark?" Pete blurted out. "Man, that doesn't seem like the best idea in the world to me, mate."

"We can handle it," Derrick grunted. "Right, Ron?"

"Fragging right," Ron nodded.

"Then what are we still standing around here for?" Danny stopped leaning against the tree, shifting his Barrett M82 around to get a better grip on it.

The squad got moving. Their pace was hurried to make the most of the light before it was lost to them. This time, it was Ron who took point. The big man led them through the trees with Danny and Derrick on his heels. Pete and Jarvis brought up the rear. Things were going to get really crappy when night fell. They didn't have any infrared gear with them. Jarvis was the only one who'd brought anything of the sort with him. He wore a pair of low light goggles about his neck.

Danny hadn't figured they would need to. The plan had never involved moving through the woods in the dark. They were supposed to have been able to set up a secure perimeter and even a few traps before the sun had set today. That just wasn't in the cards though.

Danny hadn't said anything but he had honestly, for a fleeting second, considered using Hannah's group as bait. If it had been anyone other than her he was putting at risk, Danny was forced to admit to himself that he would have done it in a heartbeat. Hannah being out here changed things though. It gave the monster just one more edge over them, as if the thing didn't have enough already. Danny knew just how strong, fast, and cunning the monster was. According to some of the stories about it, the thing had the endurance and muscle density to take damage like a living tank too. It wasn't going to be easy to kill even if they could outsmart the thing.

****

The two patrol cars pulled into the clearing where the road up into the mountains came to an end. Sheriff Levy and Warren were in the lead car, Brook and Chad in the one behind them. Following the two patrol cars was Larson's truck. Dodson had ended up riding along with Larson and her dogs. The three vehicles parked as Levy was cursing like a sailor in his mind.

There were two vans parked up here too. One was instantly recognizable as Hannah Davis's. That meant she was on a job and had taken Lord only knew how many out of towners into the woods on some sort of adventure trip. As if that wasn't bad enough, the other van appeared to be a rental. As his people got out of the patrol cars and truck, Levy paused to run the plate of the second van. It was rented out to. . .Levy stared at the screen in disbelief. Could his luck really be this bad? Shaking his head, Levy got out of the patrol car.

"What's wrong?" Brook asked.

"That van there," Levy tilted his head in its direction. "It's rented out to Daniel Harkin."

Brook's eyes went wide. "The Daniel Harkin?"

"I'd wager so," Levy frowned. "I'd heard he was back in town but with everything we've been dealing with hadn't had the chance to check in on him."

"And you think he's up here looking for trouble?" Brook asked.

Levy nodded grimly. "You can count on that."

Walking over to the van, Levy peered inside it. There was trash in the backseat and other signs that Danny hadn't come up here alone.

"The question is," Levy turned to Brook, "who did he bring with him?"

Brook didn't know what to say to that. Chad and Warren kept their mouths shut too.

Levy turned his attention to Larson and her dogs. Dodson was helping her get the dogs ready to be turned loose. There were three dogs in all. Larson was young for her career, at least she seemed that way to Levy. Most of the dog handlers his father had worked with were middle-aged, grumpy guys. Larson was way different from them in more than just her gender and age. She cared about her dogs and they were more skilled and better for it.

Trying the side door of the van, Levy found it was open. He rummaged around a bit looking for any clue as to who might be accompanying Danny Harkin. His best guess was that there were four to five people in the group, counting Danny himself. That wasn't good. Who in the hell could they be? Danny wasn't exactly well liked by the folks in Clinton. What happened to him as a kid had brought too many interested parties and unwanted attention to Clinton over the years. That meant whoever was with him likely wasn't from Clinton. Just what the hell was Danny up to anyway?

"Sheriff?" Dodson called to him, tearing Levy's attention and focus back to the here and now. "We're ready to go here."

Levy looked over at Larson and Dodson. He nodded, looking up at the sky. "Let's keep the dogs reigned in for now."

"That's what I was thinking too, sheriff," Larson smiled. "Thank you."

With Larson, Dodson and the dogs in the lead, the group got moving. Levy and Brook were in the center with Chad and Warren bringing up the rear. The sun was setting quickly. Levy was well aware how difficult and dangerous moving through the woods at night would be but they just couldn't afford to wait any longer. The other two groups likely had a lead of half a day or more on them. He felt confident that Danny and whoever he had brought along could handle themselves if they ran into trouble but couldn't say the same for Hannah and the group of tourists. If they ran into the creature up here, the odds of any of them surviving weren't good.

****

Jason, Alex, Martin, and Rachel were all exhausted by the time the sun set.

Despite their enthusiasm for the documentary they were making, none of them were used to the kind of tough hiking they'd been doing today. Hannah felt bad for them and ended up helping out with the set up of their tents. Afterwards, she got the camp's fire for the night going by herself. None of the college kids knew squat about starting one out here.

Hannah sat by the fire, warming up a pot of beans. Martin and Alex were reviewing the footage the group had shot during the day and carrying on about it. Jason had already retired into one of the tents for the night, too exhausted to do anything else. The kids had brought their own food with them and ate on the move while setting up the camp and getting settled in.

"May I sit with you?" Rachel asked, approaching Hannah.

"Sure," Hannah gave a polite smile.

Rachel took a seat across the fire from Hannah. Rachel was about ten years younger than she was, by Hannah's estimate and in her early twenties. The young woman was obviously nervous.

"You know, don't you?" Hannah asked point blank.

Shifting awkwardly, Rachel frowned and then admitted, "Yeah. Of course. It's part of why we hired you. You dated Daniel Harkin, the kid whose father and brother were supposedly killed by the creature up here. The guys are hoping you'll agree to an interview later on."

"Part?" Hannah stared at Rachel.

"You're also the most recommended guide in this entire area," Rachel explained. "You know your stuff and it shows."

"Dang straight I do," Hannah chuckled. "I ain't doing an interview though. That's not a time in my life I like to remember, much less talk about."

"I understand that," Rachel said, sounding sincere. "But. . ."

"No. . .You're not going to change my mind by telling me that my story might keep people from coming up here and getting killed or that something in it may give a clue as to how to find the creature," Hannah's voice was hard and cold. "I've been fed those lines before."

"Wait," Rachel's eyes went wide. "You don't believe in the monster, do you?"

Hannah glared at the young woman. "What does it matter?"

"It's just hard to think that someone as close to everything up here as you are wouldn't believe," Rachel said.

"Why? Like I said, I've never personally seen anything in these mountains except for some tracks and those. . ." Hannah sighed, "those could easily be faked."

"That almost sounded like you knew who was doing the faking when you said that," Rachel was hyped up now.

Hannah cocked an eyebrow but didn't answer.

Rachel sucked in a breath. "No. . .you don't. . ."

Hannah still said nothing.

"You think Daniel Harkin was behind all of it?" Rachel stammered.

Shaking her head, Hannah was quick to correct the young woman. "I didn't say that. Danny didn't kill anyone. He's a depressed and screwed up guy but he's no killer."

"I thought he joined the military," Rachel countered. "Doesn't that make him a killer?"

"Not of the sort that you are implying and he'd given up proving the monster was real by that point in his life. His inability to do that was a big part of why he left Clinton I think," Hannah shrugged. "You want the truth?"

"You know I do," Rachel begged.

"I don't know if the tracks and such that I saw up here as a kid were real or not," Hannah confessed. "For all I know, Danny could have been planting them for us to find without realizing he was doing it. Like I said, he was pretty messed up back then. But at the same time, a lot of Clinton disliked Danny so anyone could have made the tracks we found just to mess with his head. It was no secret that he was still looking for the monster back then."

"Those beans warmed up yet?" Alex asked, joining them at the fire.

"I thought you ate already," Hannah eyed him.

"I did but what can I say? I'm a growing young man," Alex grinned.

Hannah reached over to take two bowls out of the pack sitting next to her. She produced two spoons as well. Fixing a bowl for Alex and one for herself, Hannah started shoving beans in her mouth ravenously. It turned out Hannah was a lot hungrier than she had thought. The day had taken a lot out of her.

Alex ate his beans too. Rachel glanced at Alex as if she was unsure whether or not to continue with the talk they had been having before he came over to sit with them. The young woman apparently decided that what was said was going to stay between the two of them for now and was none of Alex's business, showing some respect for Hannah. Hannah was glad of it.

"What have you two been up to over here?" Alex asked, sensing that he was being left out of something.

Rachel shut him down with a quick redirect. "How did the footage turn out?"

And that was all it took. Alex's eyes lit up and he sat his beans down on the ground next to him.

"It's freaking awesome," Alex told them. "We've got all kinds of beautiful establishing shots for these woods and mountains. And everything comes across as just real and authentic as it actually is. Hey, maybe we should get some more shots before we turn in for the night!"

"No," Hannah snapped. "Creature or not, these woods are rough to move around in at night. And I'm turning in so there won't be anyone around to babysit you."

"Babysit?" Alex was clearly offended by that remark.

"Alex, you know what she means," Rachel cut in. "You know she's right too. Without her, none of us would be able to find our way anywhere out here. You really want to go stumbling about in the dark with God only knows what's out there and I'm not just talking about the creature. There are bears, wolves, and other nasty things up here too, ya know?"

Shoulders sagging in defeat, Alex was smart enough not to try to argue what Rachel said. "Fine," he frowned. "For tonight anyway. We are going to need some night shots at some point before we head back though."

"Right," Hannah grunted. "I'll keep that in mind."

Hannah finished her beans and got up. She nodded at Rachel. "Get some rest. Tomorrow will be rougher than today was. There won't be any trails at all now."

"Yes ma'am," Rachel promised.

As Hannah started for her tent, she froze. A chill ran along her spine. There was something, not human, close by among the trees. She could feel whatever it was watching them. Hannah turned around and dropped to her knees near the fire where her bag was lying.

"What the hell?" Alex blurted out.

"Hannah?" Rachel asked. "You okay?"

Her expression grim, Hannah stood back up, a hatchet in one hand, a large survival knife in the other. "We're not alone."

"Really?" Alex looked at Hannah, still sitting. "You're going to try to scare us out now?"

"Shut up," Rachel slugged him in the arm. "She's not messing around, Alex."

"There's something in the trees," Hannah told them. "Rachel, I think you're going to need to run."

A thunderous roar rang out as something bestial and hairy burst into the camp. Martin was still sitting outside of the tent he was supposed to share with Jason for the night, fiddling with a camera and seemingly editing the footage on it. Martin, trying to leap to his feet, was plowed into by the thing that came from the trees. It was like being hit by a runaway eighteen wheeler. Blood splattered into the air as Martin's bones were broken inside of him and his body was knocked aside like a rag doll cast aside by an angry child. His crumpled form rolled as it landed in the grass. The creature kept coming.

The creature didn't look anything like Hannah had ever imagined it would. She'd always thought it would be built like a tank, a hulking mass of muscle covered in brown hair. Though its form was humanoid, this thing wasn't like that. It was easy to see that it was strong as hell but its form was sleek, almost lanky. This thing didn't make her think of a Sasquatch in the normal sense at all. It reminded her more of something out of Alaskan legends. Something from a nightmare, so primal, so full of rage, that there was no human name for it. Regardless of what it was, the thing was out for blood.

Alex staggered to his feet just as the creature reached his side of the fire. A hairy hand shot out, its fingers closing around his throat. Lifting him effortlessly, the thing drew Alex to it, mouth opening to reveal jagged, yellow teeth. It bit into the side of Alex's face, tearing away a good portion of his cheek. Alex was thrashing about, legs kicking about in the air, trying in vain to break the beast's hold on him.

"Run!" Hannah shouted at Rachel.

The sound of her voice hit Rachel as if she'd been slapped. The young woman sprang up and took off out of the camp at a full sprint, legs pumping beneath her.

Snarling, Hannah launched herself at the creature. No matter how she felt about the students, they were her responsibility out here. The thing threw Alex aside, actually retreating a couple of steps, utterly surprised that someone was fighting back against it. Hannah's hatchet swung in an arc, thudding into the flesh of the creature's right shoulder with a loud thunk. She followed up by plunging her knife into its side, just below the ribs. The blade sunk in up to its hilt as the creature squealed in pain. Backhanding Hannah, the beast knocked her away to put some distance between them. Hannah managed to keep a tight enough grip on her hatchet so that she didn't lose it. Her knife was gone. Hannah hadn't been able to pull it loose. The creature did though, raging in pain and fury, and flung the weapon away. Its burning red eyes glared at Hannah as the beast raised up to its full height, standing a bit over seven feet tall. Hannah had imagined the thing being far taller from all the stories. . . especially Danny's. From how he had talked, the thing should have been a giant. That made Hannah wonder if it was just his perspective as a kid that made the beast seem that way or was this thing in front of her something completely different than what Danny had encountered?

Hannah stood facing the beast, knuckles white from the tightness of her grip on the hatchet she held, waiting for it to come at her. Alex was lying on the ground not far from her, whimpering and clutching at the mangled mess of his face. His hands were drenched red from the amount of blood he was losing. Hannah figured he was about to die.

"Hey," Jason's voice called out from behind the creature. He'd come out of his tent with a gun in hand. Hannah could see that it was a Glock. Under other circumstances, she'd be kicking his butt for bringing one along. She didn't allow weapons on her mountain tours unless things were worked out in advance. Right now though, Hannah was dang glad to see that Jason was armed.

The beast spun about, charging Jason. The Glock cracked several times in rapid succession. Jason's shots all hit the creature, hammering into its chest. The 9mm rounds didn't do much to stop it. Hell, they didn't even slow it down. The beast reached Jason, slapping the Glock from his hand. Jason screamed as his wrist was broken, knocked sideways to the point that the white of bone protruded where it bent. Before Jason could do anything else, the beast punched a fist completely through his chest. It entered just below his stomach and emerged through his back in an explosion of gore. Jason died instantly. The beast ripped its arm free from his collapsing corpse. His death had given Hannah another shot at taking the thing down herself. She raced forward, coming up on the beast's back, to leap onto it. Her left hand clutched a mass of the beast's hair, gripping it tightly, as her legs wrapped about its torso. With her other hand, Hannah struck the beast over and over with her hatchet. Each strike drew fresh blood and caused the beast to cry out in pain. The beast flung Hannah off of it. She thudded onto the ground, hatchet bouncing out of her hand. The beast was moaning from the damage Hannah had inflicted upon it but was still standing. Hannah tried to get up but a sharp pain shot through her body. Something had happened to her back when she landed, whether it was broken or simply twisted, Hannah had no idea. She couldn't move to get away from the beast. It came staggering towards her. Hannah looked around to see that Alex was either dead or unconscious and that Rachel had done as she'd been told and was gone. With Jason and Martin dead, there was no one else left to help her.

Hannah accepted her fate but wasn't going to just die without a fight. She strained to reach her hatchet but it was just beyond her grasp. Her fingers brushed against it, unable to close around it. The beast was over her now. Hannah looked up at it just in time to see the bottom of a hair-covered foot plunging downward towards her head. She heard the crunching sound of her own skull caving inward before everything went black.

****

Jarvis, Danny, Derrick, Ron, and Pete had kept moving long after the sun had set. Trudging through the woods at night wasn't exactly a super idea but they needed to put some distance between them and the civilians who were up here. Jarvis wasn't feeling it. He understood the whys of it all and knew he owed Danny his life but his gut told him that they were marching into something bad.

Danny had taken point and was leading them on at a relentless pace. Jarvis was hoping that he wasn't going to get them into trouble. He'd talked Danny into letting Derrick take the overall lead of things. . .but Derrick was keeping his mouth shut right now. If he had a problem with moving at night or their current pace, Derrick was keeping it to himself.

The plan was simple. . . to get as far as they could from the civilians that were up here and then dig in. Jarvis wouldn't have argued that at all were it not for the circumstances forcing them in the mess they were in now, on the move in the dark.

The temperature had shifted greatly from that of the day. It was actually just a touch on the chilly side. Jarvis blamed the elevation. None of them except for Danny were used to these sort of mountains. Glancing at his watch, Jarvis saw that they were about halfway through the night. None of them had stumbled and twisted an ankle or worse yet so that at least was a good thing.

Danny froze up ahead of him. Jarvis and the

others came to a stop seeing him signal them to do so. Something was wrong.

Something came bursting from the trees right at them. Pete swung the barrel of his weapon towards it but Danny leaped, slapping it down before he could fire. Jarvis saw why. It wasn't some sort of monster or creature but rather a young girl that charged them. Ron moved forward, catching the girl with one of his thickly muscled arms. The girl kicked and thrashed against Ron, screaming like a banshee.

"Calm down!" Ron bellowed at the girl. "I ain't gonna hurt you!"

The girl's eyes were wide and she was out of her head with fear. Jarvis rushed over to help before she could hurt Ron or herself.

"Hey!" Jarvis yelled at her. "Look around. It's okay. You're safe."

She seemed to hear what he was saying on some level. The girl stopped bucking about, her eyes fixed on him. "Who. . .who are you?" she whimpered.

"We're the good guys," Jarvis smirked.

Danny came over and Jarvis moved aside to let him closer to the girl.

"My name is Danny," he told her. "We're not going to let anything hurt you."

"Right," Jarvis nodded. "Like I said, you're safe."

"Now it's your turn," Danny urged the girl. "What's your name?"

"My. . .my name is Rachel," the girl managed to get out.

"And what are you running from, Rachel?" Danny pressed.

"The monster," Rachel's eyes went wide with fear again. "The monster, it killed my friends. All of them I think."

Danny didn't ask about the monster or even question her on saying there was such a thing, he knew exactly what Rachel was talking about. He'd lived through what she was going through right now himself.

"We know about the monster, Rachel," Danny assured her. "It's why we're here. We came to hunt it down and kill it."

Rachel slumped with relief in Ron's hold on her. "Oh thank God," she breathed. "Thank God."

Danny spoke carefully so as to not upset her again, "Rachel, I need to know some things from you, okay?"

She nodded.

"Can you tell me about your friends and why you're out here?" Danny asked.

"We're students at Edgar University," Rachel was trying hard to keep herself composed. "Film students. We came to make a documentary about the Clinton Monster."

Jarvis could see that what she'd said angered Danny but only because he'd known him for so long.

"Okay, Rachel," Danny was trying to keep himself calm, though Jarvis didn't know what there was to bother him. "Did you hire a guide to bring you up here?"

"Yeah," Rachel blinked. "We did. She. . .she. . ."

"Was her name Hannah?" Danny was really on edge and upset now.

Jarvis put two and two together. The guide, Hannah, had to be Danny's ex. That was what was affecting him so deeply.

"That was her name," Rachel answered, head bobbing up and down.

"Where is she now, Rachel?" Danny asked.

"I. . I don't know," Rachel stuttered.

"Think, Rachel," Danny told her, gritting his teeth. "It's important. We can't help her or your friends if you don't tell us."

"I just ran," Rachel said. "She told me to run."

Danny waited for the girl to go on.

"She. . .I think she was about to fight the creature," Rachel got out.

"What?" Danny stared at Rachel in disbelief.

"Hannah had a hatchet and a knife," Rachel said. "She was headed toward the thing. I think she was trying to save my friends."

"Damn it," Danny shook his head, turning away from Rachel.

"What ya thinking, boss?" Pete asked.

To Jarvis it looked like Danny was trying not to cry. That was something Jarvis never thought he would see after all the crap they had survived together in the service. This Hannah had to mean a lot to Danny.

"She's dead," Danny said, almost too quiet to be heard.

"Huh?" Pete cut his eyes at Ron as if looking for the big man to see if he was hearing things.

"She's dead," Danny roared, spinning around with rage in his eyes. "Is that right, Rachel?"

The girl was scared to death again, this time of Danny.

"That thing. . ." Rachel balked, "I didn't see it get her."

"But you know it, don't you?" Danny growled. "You know it murdered her."

With tears rolling down her cheeks, Rachel admitted that, "I heard screams behind me as I ran. That's all I know for sure."

Derrick stepped into the situation, positioning himself as close as he could to being between Danny and where Ron was holding Rachel.

"Ron, let her go," Derrick ordered. The big man complied quickly. Rachel stood on her own, trembling.

"Ma'am, you're going to be okay," Derrick assured her. "We will get you out of here to somewhere safe. I promise you that."

Rachel, looking relieved, gave a nod to show that she believed him.

"Derrick," Danny took a step towards him.

"Whoa now, boss," Derrick held up a hand at Danny. "I think you need to calm the frag down and get it together. Right now."

Jarvis saw that Danny was struggling not to lose it. Their former C.O. seemed about ready to have a go at Derrick for getting in his way. If that happened, the crap was really going to hit the fan. If that went down, Pete was going to side with Danny, Ron was an unknown, but he was going to have Derrick's back. Danny backed down though, storming off, without another word.

"What the frag?" Pete yelped. "Where the hell is he going?"

"Leave him be," Derrick told Pete. "He just needs a moment to get it together."

Jarvis shook his head and then found himself stepping up. "Danny will be fine, folks. What we need to worry about is the rest of us. Given that thing he's obsessed with is real. . . we need to get somewhere a hell of a lot safer than just standing around here in the dark."

No one argued with that. The group, with Rachel in tow, got moving. Danny caught up with them after cooling off.

****

Larson's dogs were going crazy, trying to get free from her grasp on their leashes. Dodson had to help her restrain them. It was strange, given how quiet they'd been since heading up into the mountains.

Levy and the rest of the group let the dogs lead them.

"What do you think they're picking up on that we aren't?" Brook asked.

"Not sure I want to know," Levy sighed but knew they had to find out.

Levy could smell smoke in the air and motioned for Chad and Warren to move ahead of the dogs in the direction it seemed to be coming from. Less than a minute later, he heard them calling out to him.

"Sheriff!" Chad yelled.

"You need to see this, sir," Warren added. "It's a fragging massacre!"

"Keep the dogs back!" Levy ordered.

Larson and Dodson remained where they were with the dogs as Levy rushed forward with Brook on his heels. They burst into a small clearing that had been a campsite. A fire still burned in its center, lighting up the area. As Levy looked around, what he saw made Warren calling it a massacre seem like an understatement. There were. . . pieces of dead people strewn all about the camp. Levy nearly stumbled over a bloody leg that looked to have been gnawed on. He'd seen crap like this before. The beast his father had tried so hard to keep secret and cover up during his time as sheriff, the creature that Brook was in such denial about, that was what had done this. Nothing else could be so ruthless, so brutal, and do this to people. An animal might kill and feed on someone, sure, but what he was seeing around him was way more than that. The thing that killed the people in this camp had utterly savaged them.

"God have mercy," he heard Brook mutter.

Chad had dropped onto his knees and was busy vomiting up the contents of his stomach. Warren was wide eyed, gawking at the carnage, one hand over his mouth, the other gripping the shotgun he carried tightly.

Levy walked closer to the fire. The upper part of a woman's body lay not far from it. One of her arms was missing. It appeared to have been violently ripped from her shoulder. Worse, her head was little more than a gory mess squished into the ground leaving no identifying features. Her clothes were torn and ripped at, breasts exposed to the night air. There was a gaping hole between them where the woman's sternum had been pulled from her chest. The white jagged tips of broken ribs poked upwards through her torn flesh. As Levy stared at her mangled corpse, he sucked in a sharp breath, realizing that he knew this woman. It was Hannah Davis.

"Is that. . .?" Brook asked from behind him.

Nodding, Levy turned to look around again before his gaze landed on Brook.

"Jeez," Brook frowned. "She was a nice lady. I always enjoyed bumping into her around town."

"Hey, boss," Warren got Levy's attention.

Levy headed over to where the deputy was.

"This guy got off some shots," Warren told him, holding a Glock he'd picked up from the ground. "Didn't do him a hell of a lot of good."

"Do we need to call this in?" Chad asked.

Levy snorted, "To who? Most of us are out here and I'm sure as hell not calling folks up here to deal with these bodies given the circumstances. These poor bastards will have to wait. Finding Danny and whatever did this takes priority. Go get Larson to bring her dogs in here."

"Yes, sir," Chad scampered off.

A moment later, the deputy returned with Dodson and Larson following after him. Larson had more tracking experience than any of them and Levy wanted her to have a look around the campsite.

Dodson held all the dogs while she did. The animals were calmer again now. It was as if the carnage spooked them too once they actually saw it and got to nose around in the campsite.

Levy could see that Larson had found something.

"Sheriff," she said, "There's the same strange tracks we've been seeing on our way up here. Big, weird things that no human or animal that I know of could have made but. . .there's another set of tracks too. I think someone escaped this mess and ran out of here like a bat out of hell."

"Then that's where we start then," Levy said. "Get the dogs on their scent and let's get going."

****

Danny bit his lip so hard that his teeth nearly cut it. He was doing his best to hold himself together but it wasn't easy. Hannah was gone. No matter how much he didn't want to believe what the girl with them had said, deep down, Danny knew it was true. He could feel it in his bones. The monster that killed his father and brother had taken her from him too. It was almost too much to deal with. The fury inside of him had blossomed into a super nova of rage. Even now, Danny barely had a grasp on it.

The formation of their group had changed a good bit since they'd gotten moving again. Ron was in the lead now on point. Jarvis was keeping close to the girl, Rachel, protecting her. Derrick brought up the rear as if he didn't trust anyone else to do that job. That left Danny walking next to Pete of all people. Pete wasn't exactly the sort one could confide in. Pete wasn't a coward but he was easily excitable with a big mouth and usually acted rashly without ever truly thinking through his actions. He was a good solider when push came to shove though and hung in there when his friends were depending on him.

Ron came to an abrupt halt, stopping everyone else in their tracks. He signaled for quiet and then for Danny to move up to join him. Danny crept towards the big man. Ron didn't need to point out what had stopped him, Danny saw it straight away. Beyond the trees in front of them was a large clearing. In its center was a large house that could be seen in the early rays of the breaking dawn. Vines grew up its sides and its walls were worn from weather but it looked very much intact otherwise.

"You think there's anyone home?" Ron whispered.

"Hell if I know," Danny shrugged, still staring at the house. It was a lot more than just a hunting cabin. Whether they still did or not, someone had lived out here. A small smokehouse sat to one side of the house and a well on the other. Danny wagered there was an outhouse somewhere around too. The place appeared to be abandoned but it could just be poorly maintained. There was no way to know for sure without the risk of approaching it closer and possibly running into some inbred hillbilly with a shotgun or worse.

"Sure would be a good place to hole up," Ron commented, letting Danny know that he was willing to take that risk.

"Can we?" Rachel pleaded. "Please. I don't want to be out here anymore. Maybe there's a phone that we can. . ."

"There's no phone," Danny said. "Not one that works at any rate. No poles for a landline and even if there was a cell, it'd be just like ours. . .without any signal this far out."

That much was clear from the lack of visible lines running into the house. There sure as hell weren't any phone poles here in the middle of nowhere.

"We need to do this," Jarvis chimed in. "In there will be a hell of a lot safer than out here."

"Hell yeah," Derrick nodded.

"Fine," Danny relented. "Jarvis, Pete, you guys take the left, we'll take the right. Let's move in and find out if anyone's home."

****

The day breathed its last and gave way to the dark. Levy was frustrated and only growing more so. The dogs still had the scent of whoever escaped the massacre at the campsite but as yet, they hadn't caught up to whoever it might be. For all the time spent marching through these cursed woods they didn't have crap to show for it.

Brook wasn't holding up much better. With sagging shoulders, she walked alongside Levy. There was a sorrowful yet fear-touched edge to her eyes since they'd stumbled onto the campsite full of ripped and gnawed upon corpses.

Dodson and Larson were out of view and ahead of the group, letting the dogs guide their way, while Chad and Warren were in the rear. From the lack of chatter and bickering between them, Levy knew the two of them were spooked too.

Not only had they failed in their attempt at catching up to whoever survived the campsite attack, there had been no sign of the beast that had done the killing either. Levy figured it was beyond questioning now that there was something not easily explained or even believed in that was out here in the woods with them.

"Sir," Brook said, drawing Levy's attention.

Levy's palm wiped at the sweat on his cheeks. The chill of the night hadn't yet erased the toils of the day. As weary as he felt, Levy turned to look at his second in command. "What is it, Brook?"

Brook's eyes again spoke for her. He could clearly see the conflict in them between accepting the truth of what they were up against out here and the insanity of even thinking such a thing. It was something he had struggled with too before finally finding acceptance that the beast of the local legends was real and his father had been covering up its existence to an extent for years, maybe even decades.

Levy didn't try to offer her any comfort. Instead, he merely said, "All the stories are real, Brook. We're going to find the thing that's out here and put it down before anyone else dies."

Giving a nod, Brook let him know that she understood.

Ahead of the group, the dogs went nuts. A cacophony of growls and barks erupted through the trees. A voice cried out. Levy couldn't tell if it was Larson or his deputy that was with her. A series of mini-claps followed, the sound of someone opening fire.

"Move!" Levy yelled at the rest of the group, surging forward in a full out sprint. As he ran, Larson's dogs came barreling past him, yipping in retreat. Levy didn't stop though and kept on plowing onward.

Bursting from the trees in the tall grass where Larson and Dodson stood, Levy saw that they were okay. . .or at least still standing. Larson was pale, eyes wide in shock and awe. Dodson was next to her, weapon aimed straight ahead of them. The deputy whirled on him as he approached.

"Whoa!" Levy shouted, saving himself from having bullets come tearing into his chest.

"Frag!" Dodson swore, lowering his gun.

The others came rushing up behind Levy as he stepped to take hold of the barrel of Dodson's AR, making sure it stayed pointed at the ground. If Dodson was offended by his action, he didn't show it. The deputy was as scared as Larson clearly was.

"It's here, Sheriff," Dodson told him. "And it's fragging huge."

"What?" Levy asked. "What's here?"

"The monster," Larson rasped.

Levy's head jerked around in her direction, surprised it was her who answered him and not Dodson.

"She's telling the truth, sir," Dodson assured him. "I saw it. Hell, I took a shot at it."

"I heard," Levy said. "Did you hit it?"

Dodson shook his head. "I don't think so. That thing is fragging fast. As soon as I pulled the trigger it was ducking back into the trees."

Chad and Warren were looking around with their guns ready to let loose on anything that moved in the shadows. Levy felt Brook place a hand on his shoulder.

"Sheriff. . ." Brook was frowning.

"Well, I guess if we needed proof that the thing

was real, we got it now," Chad huffed. Almost all of them had known Dodson long enough to know he wasn't a guy who screwed around when the crap hit the fan. If Dodson said he saw the monster then he had.

"My dogs. . ." Larson mumbled, then her voice got louder. "My dogs!"

She turned to run in the direction they had fled but Levy blocked her path, catching her.

"They're fine," he told Larson as she struggled to break his hold. "They're likely a lot safer than we are right now."

Levy felt Larson relax a little and let her go. She didn't try to go after the dogs again. Instead, she stared at him with a mixture of fear and anger on her face.

"Sir," Chad's eyes were still on the trees around them as he spoke, "I think we need to get out of here."

He was right but Levy didn't have a clue where they could go. Biting his lip, brow furrowed in thought, Levy decided their best bet was to just stay where they were. It was a hard choice to make because deep down he wanted to run away as much as Chad but it was just too risky in the dark.

"No," Levy barked. "We're staying right where we are until the sun comes up. Dodson, see if you can get a fire going. Everybody else, stay close to each other and as far away from the trees as you can."The night was long but passed without incident. No beast came to attack them. The dogs never returned though, a fact which greatly upset Larson. It was all they could do to keep her from heading out on her own in the darkness to search for them. The poor woman wore out her voice calling for them.

As the sun rose, Dodson put out the small fire that had given them some light during the night and Levy tried to take stock of their situation again. It went without saying that his deputies wanted to head back to town. . . and Larson, she was on the verge of having a breakdown with her dogs missing. Still, he was in charge and what they did fell completely upon his shoulders as sheriff. Honestly, they were too close to finding the beast to do anything but keep after it. Besides, Danny and whoever he'd brought along with him were out here somewhere too. It was his job, their job, to find Danny's group before anyone else got torn to shreds by the beast.

"Sun's up, sir," Chad huffed. "What's the plan now?"

Everyone was staring at Levy, waiting on him to give them an answer.

Levy really wished they had someone who really knew this area with them. Larson did, to an extent, but she was a mess. It was questionable if anything she said was trustworthy given her current state.

"The plan?" Levy shot back at Chad. "The plan is we do our jobs, Deputy. We know there are still people out here, whoever survived the attack on that camp and Daniel Harkin. We're not just leaving them."

No one spoke up to challenge him though everyone was either frowning or scowling. Larson was the only one to speak up at all.

"You can do what you want, Sheriff, but I'm not one of your deputies," she said as sternly as her hoarse voice would permit. "I'm going after my dogs and that's that."

Levy shook his head. "I can't let you do that. It's too dangerous out here."

"And just how are you going to stop me, Sheriff?" Larson demanded. "Throw cuffs on me?"

His expression dead serious, Levy said, "If I have to."

"Screw you," Larson gave him the finger and turned to leave.

"Chad," Levy said, voice calm and hard.

"Ma'am," Chad stepped into Larson's path. "You heard the man. Don't make us actually cuff you for your own safety."

"Please," Dodson added.

Larson ignored his plea. Lunging at Chad, she

clawed at his face hoping to drive him back in order to get past him. Being a professional who dealt with domestic situations and bar fights on a regular basis, he was ready for her. Chad caught Larson's hands and twisted her around so that they were held firmly behind her back. She struggled against him.

"You bastard!" Larson shrieked. "Let me go, damn you!"

"Quiet the hell down," Brook barked.

Larson only seemed to scream louder, letting more obscenities fly.

Brook snapped into action, knowing Larson had to be silenced before she gave away their position to everything within earshot, if that hadn't happened already. Slapping a hand over Larson's mouth, Brook bent the dog handler's head back, muffling her cries and curses. "Get me something to gag her with."

Warren produced a bandana from the pocket of his uniform and hurried to hand it to Brook who roughly wrapped it tightly around Larson's head while Chad continued to help hold the woman. With the gag in place, Brook told hold of Larson's shoulders, looking into her eyes. The gag helped but it wasn't enough to fully quiet Larson.

"I will punch you in the fragging face, woman," Brook said, giving her one last warning. When Larson still didn't shut up, Brook made good on her threat. The deputy slammed a fist into Larson's forehead, knocking the dog handler unconscious.

Chad caught Larson's dropping weight.

"Frag, Brook," he complained, "Why'd you have to knock her out? Now I am going to be stuck carrying her arse."

"Better you than me," Warren quipped as if trying to break the tension.

Levy was shaking his head sadly. "I'm sorry, Chad, but you really will be here. Leaving her here would pretty much be murder."

Chad shot Brook a glare. "Told you so. Thanks a fragging lot."

With the Larson mess resolved, Levy led the way on deeper into the woods. Chad had lifted Larson into his arms and carried her in front of him. Brook stuck close to the two of them, a bit of guilt peeking through in her otherwise determined expression. Warren brought up the rear watching for any threat that may try to sneak up on them from that direction.

Levy didn't have much faith that if the beast did attack, even in broad daylight, they would be able to see it coming. These woods were its turf after all, not theirs. This was the beast's home. One could damn well bet that the beast knew every inch of it a hell of a lot better than they did. On top of that, there was a reason memes about Sasquatch being the world's hide and seek champion existed. If the thing could stay hidden out here all the years that it had without ever truly being proven to exist, it had to be a master of stealth despite its size. As much as they tried, they would never really be ready for it out here in the open like this.

The day wore on, hot and humid. Everyone was drenched in sweat by noon and Dodson had long taken over carrying Larson. Chad just wasn't up to that task for any extended period. Warren had taken a turn too briefly but mostly kept to his position as the group's rear guard.

Levy brought everyone to a halt. All of them needed to catch their breath. Pushing too hard would only lead to screw ups and Levy was wise enough to know that.

****

Danny sat on the edge of the house's small porch. Its wood was in horrid shape. The short set of steps leading up to it were little more than barely holding together. His skin and clothes were soaked with sweat. The shirt he'd taken off lay across his knees, wet, and drying in the harsh rays of the early afternoon sun.

The house was as abandoned as it looked. Its interior was covered in dust and filth. . . and Lord only knew how many rats were living within its walls. It was safer and a lot better place to work from than Danny had ever counted on having when he'd returned to these woods though.

He looked up to see Ron approaching the house. Ron was shirtless and sweat-soaked too. Panting still from all the work he'd been doing, Ron carefully leaned against the porch's exterior railing near where Levy sat.

"Whew," Ron swiped at his brow. "We're almost done I think. Derrick and Pete are finishing up that second pit trap you wanted but that should be it."

"Good," Danny nodded with a thankful smile.

As soon as dawn broke, their entire group other than Rachel had gotten to it. Their plan all along had been to hunt the beast that was out here and trap it so they could kill the thing and make sure it was dead. This house had been a Godsend as a base of operations. They could just sit and wait on the beast to come to them now. . . and it surely would, given time. The beast didn't tolerate any intruders, as it saw them, on its land. The house made things so much easier in knowing where to set up the traps too. The perimeter around the house was a field of hidden death ready to dish out pain to anything that stumbled into it. They hadn't stopped there though. There were a few surprises inside the house as well.

Rachel emerged through the house's front door

behind where Danny was sitting. He had been rather an A hole to Rachel when the group had found her and was still far from her favorite person. They managed to bury the hatchet, so to speak, between them enough to be civil though.

The house had a working generator which Pete had got running so they had lights and running water. And it was a tray of water glasses that Rachel was bringing out of the house. None of them had asked her to pitch in with the work they were doing so apparently Rachel had taken it upon herself to at least contribute in some fashion.

"You want some water?" Rachel asked. "You look like you could use some."

Both Danny and Ron accepted the glasses she offered them, returning her smile with ones of their own.

"Thanks," Ron nodded at Rachel after taking a swig.

Danny scanned the trees surrounding the house, scowling.

Ron must have noticed because he said, "Finding this place was quite the break to catch, eh? Things are finally coming together so that we can get started on killing that beastie of yours."

Unable not to chuckle a bit, Danny brought a fist up to his lips to at least muffle the sound of it.

"You guys honestly knew that thing was out here?" Rachel asked.

"You ran into us hunting it, didn't you?" Ron smirked.

There hadn't really been a lot of time for them to talk until now.

"Yeah," Rachel cocked her head sideways, "I guess I did and thank God for it."

"Hey," Danny drew her attention, "Look. . .I'm sorry about how I was when you ran into us. Just. . .it's just that killing this thing means a great deal to me and I didn't want anything slowing us down or screwing up our chance to take a shot at it."

"Sort of some kind of revenge thing I'm guessing?" Rachel asked.

"It's personal," Danny said and left it at that.

"What I don't understand is that if y'all knew that thing was real and out here killing people. . ." Rachel started.

"Why didn't we warn folks?" Danny finished for her. "Trust me, I spent years trying to. No one would listen to me. People just don't want to believe things like this monster are real."

Rachel let the subject drop, glancing at Ron. "And what about you? Is it personal for you too?"

Ron laughed. "Not at all. I just owe that bastard sitting there my life. He asked for help and I couldn't say no."

"So what are guys, soldiers or something?"

Rachel looked back at Danny but it was Ron who answered her.

"We were once," he said with an almost sad tone in his voice.

At that moment the radio sitting next to Danny crackled to life.

"Hey boss man!" Pete's voice called out. "We got incoming."

Danny leaped to his feet, snatching up his high powered rifle. They had redistributed all the weapons and placed those not being used at strategic places throughout the house and just inside both its front and rear doors. Their ammo supply had been dealt out in the same manner. Doing so allowed all of them to adjust what they were carrying if they wanted to. Danny was packing a .50 caliber BMG now. Even as big and tough as his monster was, he figured a single shot would still tear it a new one.

Before Danny could go charging in the direction that Pete and Derrick were supposed to be working, Pete's voice rang out again.

"It's not your monster though, boss," Pete informed them.

"What?" Danny barked back over the radio.

"We got people out here," Pete responded. "Looks like the whole bloody sheriff department of that little town we met up in."

"Frag," Danny growled, rage boiling up inside

of him. The bastard sheriff must be after him. He couldn't think of anything else that would have dragged Levy and his people out here in such force.

"What do you want us to do?" Pete asked.

"Stay where you are and keep an eye on them," Danny ordered. "I'm coming to you."

Lowering the radio, Danny turned to Ron.

"Yeah," Ron was already saying, "I know. Stay here and keep this place safe."

"If it's the cops, they can help us, can't they?" Rachel was confused and almost frantic.

"Just stay here with Ron for now," Danny told her. "Everything's going to be okay."

Rachel did as he said even though she was on the edge of bolting along with him. Danny left her and Ron behind, legs pumping beneath him as he ran. The pit Pete and Derrick were finishing up wasn't that far away. Jumping over bunches of thick roots that protruded from the ground at the base of some larger trees and ducking low lying limbs, Danny moved as fast as he could, slowing only when his two friends came into sight. He came to a stop behind the trunk of a tree, using it as cover, as Derrick motioned for him to stay where he was. Danny froze watching Derrick, who signaled for him to look towards their east. Danny did.

In the distance was a group of six people, five

of them in sheriff department uniforms and the sixth dressed like a civilian. That sixth person was a woman in her later twenties or early thirties based on what he could see of her. She was either unconscious or dead as one of the uniformed officers was carrying her limp body in his arms.

Signaling Pete and Derrick that he was going to approach the group, Danny crept through the trees, keeping hidden, and moving as quietly as he could until finding a spot he felt comfortable calling out to them from.

"What brings you out here, Sheriff?" Danny bellowed, hoping the acoustics of the woods would stop them from instantly knowing where he was.

The group reacted much like he expected them to. The officers, all except for the one carrying the woman, raised their weapons and fanned out, scanning the trees around them, trying to catch a glimpse of whoever had called out to them.

"That you Danny?" Sheriff Levy shouted.

"I don't want any trouble, Sheriff," Danny responded.

"We're not looking for any either, Danny," the Sheriff answered. "But I need you put down your gun and come out where I can see you. Your buddies too."

Danny knew the sheriff couldn't see him but had taken an educated guess that he'd be armed. As to knowing how he wasn't alone, Danny had no idea how the sheriff knew that.

"We both know that's not going to happen, Sheriff," Danny snarled. "I've got business to finish out here. After that. . ."

"I'd say we have the same business," Sheriff Levy snapped. "Put down your gun and come on out. We can deal with the thing that's running around out here together."

"So you admit that the monster is real now, all of a sudden?" Danny huffed.

"I do," the sheriff answered. "We can help each other, Danny. You gotta trust me."

"Yeah, not happening, Sheriff. I've been down roads like that before and every time I've gotten screwed."

"I'm not my father, Danny," the sheriff assured him.

Danny was honest. "Trusting you is a risk I can't afford to take."

"Then I am afraid that leaves us in a really bad predicament, Danny, because I can't let you and your friends stay out here on your own."

"I haven't broken any laws," Danny said 'I' instead of 'we' so as not to confirm for the sheriff that he wasn't alone.

"I imagine you and your buddies are packing some serious firepower that you don't have all the paperwork on," the sheriff pointed out.

"Even if we were that's a pretty desperate play,

Sheriff," Danny laughed.

"If I leave here and you get yourself torn apart, that's on me, Danny, and I can't live with that," the sheriff motioned at those with him.

Danny saw the signal and knew what was happening. The sheriff and his deputies were about to break and fan out, hoping to flank him. Danny didn't want to open fire on them but wasn't left with any other option that he could think of. Before he could even raise his BMG 50 though, Pete and Derrick sealed everyone's fates, plunging them all into a desperate firefight. Pete's M4 rained death down at the sheriff and his deputies. Danny cursed inwardly. Pete was shooting not to drive them off or wound them but to kill. There would be hell to pay for that later if any of them survived all this insanity and made it out of these woods alive.

One of the deputies screamed in pain and went down, blood spurting from his right side. The others all managed to make it to cover and were returning fire. Pete and Derrick's attack had given away their position. Bullets ripped into the trees around the two of them. Danny saw Derrick take a hit. Though it didn't look as if the round that struck him did more than graze Derrick's arm, he dropped his weapon nonetheless. The ground Pete and Derrick were on was slightly elevated in comparison to where the sheriff and his people were. Derrick's gun slid just enough along the incline to be beyond his reach without him giving up what cover he had. They were pinned down by the amount of fire coming their way. Danny had no choice but to intervene.

Danny's BMG 50 wasn't exactly designed to be used in a firefight but he shouldered the weapon anyway. A single hit from the heavy weapon would reduce a good portion of a human being to red mist. Danny still didn't want to kill the sheriff and his people, aiming carefully to avoid that while at the same time letting them know the level of firepower they were up against.

The BMG 50 thundered. The shot Danny fired slammed into the trunk of a tree near one of the deputies. The wood blew apart in a shower of splinters. The deputy wailed as they tore into his flesh.

"Frag it," Danny muttered, lowering the big gun. He hadn't intended to hurt the deputy but just blow apart the tree trunk for some shock and awe.

The shot gave away his position and the sheriff himself sent a shotgun blast into the woods at him. The slug missed Danny but only narrowly. Then everything really did go to hell in a hand basket.

In utter disbelief, Danny saw the beast charging through the trees, low lying limbs snapping as the thing moved through them like a high speed tank. It was on Pete and Derrick before they even fully realized what was happening. Derrick turned toward the beast as the thing's giant hands clasped onto him, lifting his entire body effortlessly into the air. The beast tore Derrick apart, entrails and blood splattering outward in an explosion of gore as his body separated, down the middle, into two halves. Derrick's unfortunate end bought Pete time enough to swing his M4 around. Pete's finger worked the trigger rapidly, the carbine cracking over and over, as the semi-auto rounds hammered the monster at almost point blank range. The beast was so enraged that it somehow ignored the force of the impacts and the pain it had to be feeling, forcing itself on, forward, at Pete. A swipe of its claws shredded the soft flesh of Pete's face from the top of his forehead to his chin, leaving wide, red gaps spraying blood. Pete stumbled backwards, giving a wet sounding cry, as his own blood flooded his mouth from his mangled lips. The beast struck again with blinding speed, plunging a hair-covered fist deep into Pete's abdomen. As the fist came back out of Pete's body it clutched a wad of squished intestines. Pete tumbled sideways, flopping onto the ground. The beast lunged, bringing a huge foot downward onto his head. Pete's skull popped like an overripe melon beneath the beast's weight.

"No!" Danny howled, aiming his BMG 50 at the beast which had just slain his friends. taking aim at the beast which had just slain his friends with his BMG 50. Before he could fire, the thing leaped down the incline, powerful legs pumping like pistons as it ran towards the sheriff and his deputies. Danny didn't have a clear shot at it. Cursing, he hurried to shift his own position.

The sheriff and his people certainly saw the beast coming. The thing let out a roar that seemed to shake the very trees themselves. A female deputy was blazing away at the monster with an AR while the sheriff's shotgun boomed. None of it was stopping the thing though. It reached the area where the sheriff and his people were, rushing the closest of them. The poor bastard had his head jerked from his shoulders and flung away into the trees.

Danny finally got a shot at the monster. His BMG 50 thundered. The .50 caliber round it fired streaked through the air like a super sonic missile. . .and yet, the bullet missed its target. The trunk of a small tree blew apart in a shower of wooden shards. The beast had leaned over in preparation to pounce at its next victim just enough to be out of the bullet's path.

Still, the shot spooked the creature. Realizing that another shot might be coming its way, the beast whirled about and plowed a path into the trees away from the sheriff and his people.

Danny rushed halfway down the incline,

shouting, "This way before it comes back! Hurry!"

The sheriff wasn't an idiot. He let the argument between them go and led his people after Danny who called back over his shoulder, "Follow me exactly. We've got traps set up all over the place."

"Traps," the sheriff muttered, shaking his head as he ran. "Just fragging great."

****

Sheriff Levy had found both his "monsters" or rather, they had found him. . .and now, one was saving him from the other.

"Damn you, Danny," Levy swore quietly. No one heard him through the chaos. They were all sprinting after Danny, trying to keep up with him.

"This way," Danny shouted, changing course. Levy had been on his heels but slowed his pace to fall back. After watching Dodson so brutally killed by the monster, he was determined not to let any more of his people be hurt by it. Levy let Brook, Chad, who was red-faced and hurting from the effort it took to carry Larson with him, and Warren pass by. The monster was dangerously close to him. He could smell the thing's foulness, a heavy animal musk combined with the scents of blood and human entrails that smeared its hair.

Levy had already chambered another round in

his shotgun. He wanted to blast the beast, head on, but knew that would be akin to suicide. If he stopped any longer than he already had, the thing would be on him and he'd be dead. Levy poured on the speed again, pushing himself on as hard and fast as he could. Unfortunately Levy lost sight of the others. They'd disappeared from view ahead of him among the trees. He could only head in the direction that was his best guess at which way they went.

Ahead of him Levy saw that the ground. . .wasn't right. There was something off about it. Pushing himself even harder, Levy put every ounce of strength and will inside of him into a leap, praying to land on the other side of it. He came up short, landing just at the edge of the odd patch of ground. It gave way beneath him as the limbs covered with torn up chunks of grass and earth fell downwards. His fingers caught the edge of the pit that had opened up. It hurt like hell as the weight of his body came down on them but Levy held tight. In the pit below was a sea of wooden spikes, pointing upwards. The monster came barreling along behind him. Though the thing saw the pit, its mass and momentum was far too great to be brought to such a quick halt. The beast plunged into the pit, landing amid the spikes. Some of them snapped and broke under the monster but others pierced its body. The beast gave an animal squeal of pain, flopping about. Doing so only made things worse for it as more spikes slid through its thick hair into its body. Levy watched as the beast forced itself back onto its feet with an angry roar. Bright patches of red were all over its body and most of them still had pieces of wooden spikes sticking out of them. It was almost unbelievable that the thing had survived and not just survived but was actually staggering towards the edge of the pit that he clung to. Levy grunted with effort, attempting to pull himself up and roll his body out of the pit but he wasn't strong enough. He looked back at the beast and their eyes met. The primal rage that burned within the beast's eyes scared the hell out of Levy. It was something he'd never be able to forget, no matter how he tried, for the rest of his life. Those eyes would haunt him in his nightmares every night until he died.

Suddenly, a pair of boots knocking dirt over the edge onto him drew his attention. Danny had appeared at the edge of the pit above him, his hulking rifle aimed downward at an angle towards the approaching beast.

"Die, you bastard," Danny said through gritted teeth and then squeezed the weapon's trigger. The high powered rifle cracked so loudly that Levy shook his head against the pain in his ears. The bullet Danny fired struck the beast, dead on, in the center of its chest, punching a double fisted-sized hole through its torso. The beast took one final, staggering step and then collapsed back onto the spikes. Its corpse lay there twitching as blood ran freely from its numerous wounds.

"Hang on," Danny barked, laying his rifle down in the dirt at the pit's edge, in order to offer Levy a hand. Levy grabbed it and let Danny help him up and out of the pit.

Once he was out of the pit, Levy turned to stare down at the monster's bloodied form alongside Danny.

"That was a long time coming," Danny said.

Levy wasn't sure if Danny was talking to him or just expressing his thoughts out loud. Either way, Levy opted to say, "This was very personal for you, wasn't it?"

Danny's head swung around so that he could meet Levy's eyes.

"You damn well know that it was," Danny snarled but then frowned. "Look, I'm sorry, man. You're not your father and I shouldn't be piling my crap with him onto you."

"I guess all that really matters is that the thing's reign of terror up here is finally over," Levy pointed out.

"Amen to that," Danny smiled. It was his first real smile in a long, long time.

Something moved in the woods on the other

side of the pit making both of them look towards the noise. Levy gawked in disbelief as a creature taller and more muscled than the thing Danny had just killed emerged from the trees. The beast's hair was spattered with patches of gray. He heard Danny swallow hard, just as in shock as he was. The thing stared back at them, red eyes full of rage. Raising a hand, the beast thumped its chest and let out a whooping cry. From the trees behind it came more like the one Danny had killed. . .lots more.

"Dear God in heaven help us," Levy pleaded.

"Run!" Danny yelled, snapping off a hurried shot with his rifle. He missed the leader of the creatures but hit one of those behind it. The wounded monster shrieked in pain as a chunk was blown out of its right shoulder. Collapsing to its knees, the beast tried to place its hand over the carnage but the bloody mess was too big to be covered completely.

The leader of the beasts roared and threw an arm in the direction of Danny as if ordering those with it to attack. That action scared Levy more than anything. It indicated that the things were even smarter than he suspected the first beast had been.

Levy ran like hell with Danny on his heels. The creatures surged forward after them, coming around both sides of the pit where their brother creature lay dead.

"Watch out for the traps!" Danny warned, catching up to Levy.

The two men fled, knowing that sooner rather than later, the huge beasts would overtake them. The things were impossibly fast and agile for their size.

The beasts spread out as they came. Levy thought he saw Danny grin as they saw that. He got the feeling that Danny had quite a few surprises in store for the monsters chasing them. . . and he wasn't wrong.

One beast set off a tripwire that loosed a low lying limb that had been pinned back with a great deal of tension. It sprang towards the beast, driving a sharpened stake into the creature's stomach. Splinter-covered wood tore at the guts inside its body as the beast struggled to free itself and pull the stake out. Levy didn't know if the blow would be enough to kill the creature but it sure did the trick of slowing it down.

A burly Sasquatch ran smack through an area where the ground was covered in concealed Punji sticks. The pointed sticks shredded the flesh of its lower legs. Rivers of red ran from its multiple wounds. The beast, howling, whirled about wildly, trying to figure out how to escape the mess it had gotten into but ended up impaling one of its giant feet upon a Punji stick. Shrieking like an animal driven mad from pain, the beast jerked the stick out of its foot, doing more damage to itself in the process.

Another beast triggered a second tripwire but the loosed limb that swept violently at it didn't fully hit its target. The beast tried to dodge, hurling its massive body sideways. The result was the stake at the end of the limb sunk into the thick muscle of its upper arm rather than burying itself in the thing's guts. Yanking the stake out, the beast snarled and resumed its charge after Danny and Levy.

The traps were slowing the creatures so far but there were just so many of the fragging things. Levy hoped like hell that Danny knew where he was going. He followed the half-crazed vet through the woods until he could see a clearing through the trees where an old house stood. The two of them burst out of the woods sprinting towards it as behind them something blew. One of the beasts had stepped on what must have been a fragging land mine. Where the frag Danny had gotten that level of ordnance Levy didn't have a clue. Danny could have somehow made the thing himself for all he knew. Regardless, the exploding device did its job. The beast that triggered the mine was blown to bits, bits of its body spinning through the air within a shower of splattering red gore. That beast wasn't the only one hurt by the blast though. It knocked two others from their feet. The rest of the creatures stopped their mad charge somewhere within the trees. Levy couldn't see any of them anymore as he stole a glance back over his shoulder.

"Watch the steps!" Danny ordered as the two of them neared the house.

Jumping over to them to land on the porch itself, Danny turned, jerking up the barrel of his BMG 50 towards the woods. Levy made it onto the porch after him.

"Come on!" Brook urged Levy, standing just inside the house's front door with a man that Levy didn't recognize.

Levy darted inside. Danny followed and slammed the door shut behind him.

****

Inside the house was chaos. The deputies and the ex-soldiers didn't really know what to make of each other. There was immediate distrust and dislike between them. All of them knew that the real threat was outside though and that kept them from tearing into one another. As Danny and Levy made it inside, both seemed to think they were in charge.

"Get this door barricaded!" Levy shouted.

"Check the rear of the house!" Danny barked.

"Where are. . .?" Ron started but Danny stopped

him.

"Derrick and Pete are dead," Danny said. "One of those things tore them apart."

"What?" Ron stammered, having heard exactly what Danny said. "What do you mean 'things'?"

"There's more than one of those beasts out there," Levy snapped. "God only knows how many."

"Danny?" Ron looked at his C.O. for confirmation.

Nodding, Danny answered, "I killed one of them. That's when the crap really hit the fan out there."

Ron went green, putting a hand over his mouth.

"Don't you dare throw up, mate," Jarvis nudged him. "We don't have time for that right now."

Then Jarvis followed Danny's order, taking off for the rear of the house to make sure the backdoor was secure and check out the situation there. Ron appeared to pull himself together and went after him. That left Danny and Rachel alone with Levy and those in his group.

Danny's eyes took them all in for a second, sizing them up. The sheriff was a tough bastard, he'd seen that much already. It was easy to pick out who his second in command was. The lady deputy, Brook, had her crap together and was trying to keep the other woman in cuffs and civilian clothes from losing it anymore than she already was. The woman was trying desperately to get free. The sheriff's other deputies, a pair of guys named Chad and Warren, had scooted a couch up to the front door, putting weight against it and then split apart, each heading to one of the windows that were in the room facing the house's front yard.

"I don't see any sign of those things, boss!" Chad yelled.

"Clear over here too," Warren added.

Danny's men hadn't called out in warning from the rear so he assumed it was secure for the time being.

Levy stepped up to him. Danny and the sheriff found themselves in a glaring match.

"Danny," Levy said, "We're gonna have to work together or none of us are gonna survive this."

"I got no issue working with you, Sheriff, but I've spent my life chasing one of these monsters. I know a hell of a lot more about them than you do and I ain't taking orders from someone who doesn't know crap, sheriff or not."

Levy gritted his teeth, "Now hold up, dang it. . ."

"I get that you have authority, man, I do. That still doesn't change the reality of the mess we're in. No matter what you think you know about these things, I can promise you that I know more," Danny swore. "You want us to survive, you're going to have to listen to me. The rest we can settle up when we make it back to town. Hell, I'll surrender myself then if I need to."

A few seconds passed before Levy answered, "Fair enough. This is your show for as long as it has to be."

Danny nodded, glad to have avoided a fight that he'd been afraid was almost certainly coming.

"Alright, Danny," Levy eyed him, "what do we do now? Just how in the Hell are we going to get back to town?"

"We can't get out of here," Danny sighed. "We're just as trapped as I am wagering you already knew we were before you even asked that question. On the upside, my boys and I laced as much of the woods around this place with traps as we could. You saw them. They should be hurting those fragging things right now. Lord willing, it'll cut down their numbers some."

"Can't count on it though," Levy countered.

"I think we can to an extent," Danny shot back. "The question is just how many of those things there are."

"There can't be that many," the lady deputy, Brook, chimed in.

"You think?" Danny gave a wry grin. "Up until a few minutes ago, I thought there was only one and like I said, I've spent most of my life trying to prove the thing existed and hunt it down."

"So you're saying what? That there could really be an army of those things up here in these mountains?" Brook scoffed. "I don't buy that."

Outside the house, a chorus of howls and shrieks arose. They were coming from just about every direction. It was impossible to tell just how many different voices there were among the cries.

"There's your answer," Danny said gruffly. "Army or not, there are a hell of a lot more than we can handle if we just go trying to march our way out of here."

"Those things are so fast and strong," Rachel said. "Are we even safe where we are?"

Danny shook his head. "If those things make a real push to get in here, they will, no matter what we do."

"You make it sound like we're dead already," Brook commented.

"No, we're not. What I mean is we can't afford to make even a single mistake with those creatures. One screw up could cost us everything," Danny explained.

"What the frag are they doing?" Chad looked at him and Levy. "Why aren't they just coming at us already?"

Danny grunted. "The traps. They must have gotten fragged up enough to make them be a bit more cautious."

"That won't last though," Levy pointed out.

"No," Danny agreed. "It won't."

****

Hours had passed since everyone had holed up in the house, surrounded by the beasts. The night was cooler than the day but it was still muggy within the wooden walls. Jarvis was on the current watch with the female deputy, Brook. Everyone else, except Danny on watch upstairs, was trying to get some rest. Most were resting in the living room, spread out on its chairs and the couch. The crazy acting woman that kept yelling about her dogs had been taken to one of the rooms adjoining the living room, gagged, and left tied up there.

The back of the house was pretty dang secure. The only rear door was not only barricaded but they had also boarded it up. In addition, Danny had set up a nasty surprise for anything that managed to get through it. . . as well as a few other smaller surprises in the kitchen area too.

There was just no way to keep an eye on all the windows downstairs. They had done what was possible for them but that wasn't much. As thus, he and Brook were focused on the front door and the two windows near it. He stood at one, Brook at the other. They were close enough where they could talk quietly as long as they kept their voices low.

"What a fragging mess, eh?" Jarvis half chuckled.

At first, Brook just shook her head but then finally she responded, "It's sure not how I thought my weekend was going to go."

Brook managed a weak, wry grin to accompany what she said.

That made him laugh. . . a real laugh. He needed it too. It broke the tension between them as well.

"So what's your story?" Brook asked.

"Oh you know, best friend calls you up and says, hey come help me blow the hell out of the monster that ate my family and you can't tell him no. Just the same old, same old," Jarvis smiled.

"Seriously?" Brook stared at him.

"Pretty much," Jarvis nodded. "We all served together. Danny was our C.O., saved our butts more than a few times."

"And that's why you owe him," Brook commented.

Jarvis nodded again. "Danny might be screwed up but really we all are. War does that to folks. Thing is, Danny was screwed up before the war. Honestly, I think it helped put him back together, sort of."

"Now that's messed up," Brook frowned.

"Can't argue that," Jarvis shrugged. "Don't suppose it matters. We're all killers. We were trained to be that, so when Danny asked for help. . ."

"I get it," Brook said. "At least I think I do."

"What about you?" Jarvis turned her original question back at her.

"Just another day on the job," Brook quipped.

Jarvis smirked, cocking his head slightly sideways.

"We heard your former C.O. was back in town. My boss figured he was looking for trouble and dragged just about the entire department out here to find him but instead, we stumbled onto a bunch of dead kids first."

"I bet they were Rachel's friends," Jarvis interjected. "Rachel was with them when one of those things attacked their camp, barely got away. If she hadn't run into us, Rachel would likely be dead now."

"Glad you were there to save her," Brook said. "Enough folks have died already."

Real sorrow dripped from her words.

"You lost someone?" Jarvis frowned.

"Dodson," Brook answered and then explained. "He was one of us deputies. Worked with him for years. Good guy."

"Good friend too from the sound of it," Jarvis added.

"Yeah," Brook nodded.

Jarvis didn't know how to comfort her. He had

certainly known enough loss. He'd seen so much of it during his time in the service. Still, everyone dealt with it differently.

"Never in my life did I think I would find myself stuck in an old, run down house surrounded by a tribe of killer Sasquatch," Jarvis said, changing the subject.

His remark made Brook grin again. "Yeah, me either."

"All of us except the girl, Rachel, are no strangers to violence," Jarvis met Brook's eyes. "And we sure as hell have some firepower on our side too."

"You think it'll be enough?" Brook asked.

"Hell if I know," Jarvis smiled. "I was just trying to make myself feel better about this crap."

He and Brook were really hitting it off. Jarvis could feel a connection growing between them. Unsure how he felt about that, Jarvis sighed and looked out at the distant trees.

The night was intensely dark. The moon and stars had been obscured by thick clouds. Even squinting, Jarvis's eyes couldn't pierce the shadows. The Sasquatch had been quiet for a while now but he knew they were still around. Only a fool or an idiot would think otherwise. The creatures were merely biding their time, waiting for the perfect moment to strike. It felt like they were the cat and he and the others were mice.

"So what about your boss?" Jarvis nodded his head towards where the sheriff was asleep in the living room behind them.

"What about him?" Brook shrugged.

"Does he have a stake in this too?" Jarvis pressed her, "I mean beyond just doing his job as sheriff."

"His dad was the sheriff before him," Brook said. "I think there's some crap he's dealing with there but I don't know any more than that."

Jarvis wasn't sure if he fully believed her but didn't press Brook any further on it.

Sheriff Levy stirred where he was in the recliner near the rear of the living room. He got up from it and started toward them as if somehow talking about him had summoned the sheriff to them.

"Sit rep?" Levy rubbed at his eyes, apparently trying to fully wake up.

"Those things aren't even moving around out there," Brook told him.

"At least not that we can hear or see anyway," Jarvis's focus had returned to the woods outside.

Sheriff Levy grunted. "I suppose that's good. At dawn, we need to try to get the hell out of here."

Jarvis flinched at that.

"I am well aware that's not what Danny wants," Sheriff Levy stared at him. "But you damn well know just as much as I do that staying here is just as good of a way to get killed. If we're on the move, we've at least got a chance of surviving this mess," the sheriff growled.

Jarvis knew that Danny wasn't leaving until all the monsters were dead but opted to keep that to himself.

"I hear ya," was all he said back to the sheriff.

****

Upstairs, Danny sat alone in a corner bedroom that gave him a full view of two sides of the house. He had pulled a wooden chair up to the window and sat in front of it. The window was open and the breeze that blew in through it was cooler than Danny would have expected. It chilled him and made Danny shiver. He clutched the BMG 50 in his hands a bit tighter and raised the weapon up to look through its scope. The night was too dark outside to see much without it. The scope on the rifle was a Latitude 10-40X60 modified to have a low light feature. With it, Danny scanned the trees. There wasn't a lot to be seen. The woods were quiet too, almost eerily so given how loud the beasts had been earlier.

The shock that there was more than a single beast still had Danny's mind reeling on an emotional level. All his life, he had wanted vengeance on the beast that killed his father and brother. And now he had. . . or rather, Danny had killed one of them. He had no means of knowing if it was "the" creature or not. That left Danny wondering just what in the hell he was supposed to do now? Declare war on the entire tribe of things that lived out here or take the victory all achieved and call it over? Shooting the bastard monster in the pit was one of the most moving moments in his life. In that moment, he had felt closure and peace, having finally avenged his family only to have it ripped from him as the other monsters revealed themselves.

Danny's knuckles went white as his grip on the BMG 50 grew tighter. Teeth pressed together in frustration, he leaned closer to the window. Danny didn't have any answers. All he had was a burning anger raging inside of him. Inhaling a deep breath, Danny exhaled it slowly then scanned the trees surrounding the house again through the BMG 50's scope. He was thirsty for more Sasquatch blood. There was still nothing to see in his field of view. Muttering a quiet curse, Danny was about to lower his rifle but caught a hint of movement in the shadows. It was subtle. Questioning if what he saw was even real or just in his mind, Danny stared intently at the spot among the shadows of the woods where he thought the movement had been. There was only darkness and trees. Then everything went to hell faster than the clap of the starting shot of a race.

From seemingly out of nowhere, the monster came. The thing was massive, built like a tank, all muscle and hair. Eyes burning with red rage, its thick legs pumped with ferocious speed. Bounding across the small clearing between the house and the woods, it came directly towards the house's front door.

Danny jerked upright where he sat, trying to get off a shot at the monster. The BMG 50 thundered but the monster was too fast. Danny's shot missed it entirely and then it was too close to the house and out of his line of fire. He heard the wood-shattering smash of the monster colliding with the door downstairs. Danny couldn't do a damn thing about that though. His attention was jerked back to the woods as a chorus of furious cries erupted in the darkness. As he looked at the trees now, Danny saw a half dozen, maybe more, of the monsters emerging from them. His BMG 50 was the only weapon any of them had that could likely stop one of the creatures with a single shot. That was why he had taken the upstairs watch, to pick off what of the monsters he could before they reached the house. Danny swung the heavy rifle to take aim at one of the creatures as they all moved towards the house. The BMG 50 roared again and this time, the shot he fired found its target. The round slammed into a Sasquatch that stood almost eight feet tall. Blood exploded into the night air in a red mist as the Sasquatch's chest caved inward and a giant exit hole was blown through its back. The Sasquatch stumbled, dead on its feet, and collapsed, bouncing along the ground, carried on by its own momentum. Danny rushed to get a bead on another of the monsters and then fired again. The head of a Sasquatch blew apart in a shower of gore and bone fragments. Readying himself and the rifle to go for another shot, the floor beneath Danny's feet shook. It was enough to cause him to fall out of the chair he was sitting in. Danny thudded to the floor, onto his back, the barrel of his BMG 50 swinging upwards as he unintentionally discharged the weapon. It punched a gaping hole through the roof above him. Dust and small chunks of wood fell onto him where he lay.

Below him, downstairs, all hell had broken loose. A cacophony of gunfire and screams had erupted. Danny could tell that the others were in trouble. He had to get down there and help them. His chance at stopping the creatures from up here was over with anyway. Leaping up from the floor, Danny paused only long enough to eject the magazine of his BMG 50 and slam a fresh one home, then he charged out of the bedroom, heading for the stairs.

****

Brook's eyes bugged as she sucked in a startled breath. The night had been quiet and still, then in the span of a heartbeat, there was a giant monster lunging from the woods on a collusion course with the house.

"Holy frag!" Jarvis shouted.

Both of them brought their weapons to bear on the charging beast as behind them, Sheriff Levy started yelling to wake up the others. Brook's AR-15 chattered, spent shell casings clattering to the wooden floor at her feet. Jarvis was armed with an M4, constantly switching out weapons since they got to the house. It blazed away at the hulking beast on full auto. Bullets tore and ripped at the creature, most inflicting no real damage. The density of its muscle kept the rounds from doing more. If anything the barrage seemed to only make the beast angrier. There was just no stopping it. The beast barreled straight into the front door. Neither the door nor the furniture shoved up to it as a makeshift barricade could stand against it. The door was shattered into flying pieces of broken wood and splinters and the barricade knocked aside. With a roar, the beast kept right on going deeper into the house, though it did have to duck down with the upper portion of its body. Poor Warren, who had just come running out of one of the downstairs rooms where he'd been asleep, found himself in the beast's path.

Large, hair-covered hands seized him. Warren's rifle thudded onto the floor, jarred from his grasp, as the beast lifted him effortlessly, smashing his head into the ceiling. The deputy died instantly from the brutal force of the impact of his skull against the wooden boards.

Sheriff Levy's shotgun boomed. The heavy slug it fired blew open the Sasquatch's stomach. Strands of purple, red-slicked entrails poured out from the wound. The Sasquatch howled and swung Warren's corpse like a bat at the sheriff who was knocked from his feet. With the sheriff down, the Sasquatch spun to face Jarvis and Brook.

"Frag you!" Jarvis raged, advancing towards the beast, his M4 still blazing. He was aiming for the thing's face and peppering it with rounds. They slashed at the beast's cheeks and forehead. One lucky shot punched into the beast's right eye, reducing it to a red pulp inside its socket. The beast took a swing at Jarvis. A huge, clawed hand lashed out. Jarvis tried to dodge but the beast's claws managed to rake across the top of his right arm. Their sharp tips shredded his flesh as Jarvis cried out.

Brook moved to try and draw the beast's attention to her.

"Hey!" Brook shouted furiously, finger working the trigger of her AR-15, as she put a trio of rounds into the center of the beast's chest. They were just as ineffectual as the earlier rounds that had hit it from her rifle. The beast paid her no attention though, despite Brook's effort. Its fury was relentlessly directed at Jarvis.

The former soldier, having dropped his M4, drew a long knife, sheathed on the side of his boot. Jarvis's blade gleamed in the dim starlight that spilled into the house as the Sasquatch grabbed at him. Plunging the knife into the Sasquatch's upper left arm, Jarvis buried it there to the hilt. The Sasquatch roared in pain and anger. Chad, who had joined the battle, blasted the beast in the back with his shotgun. The shot made the beast lurch forward, blood pouring from the mangled hole Chad had blown in it. Whirling about, the Sasquatch's huge hand swept through the air, striking Chad with enough force that his head was removed from his neck. It flew across the room, thudding into a far wall, before bouncing onto the floor. Chad's headless corpse, blood spraying from the stump of its neck, staggered a few steps and then toppled over.

Sheriff Levy finished the beast, stepping right up to the thing, pressing the barrel of his shotgun to the softer flesh of its throat and squeezing the trigger. The beast's neck was reduced to a mass of mangled red meat. The sheriff barely managed to get out of the way as its massive body fell over.

A crash sounded in the room just off of the

living room where they'd left Larson tied up. Brook knew that the dog handler would be helpless, bound as she was, and just leaving her to die was basically murder. Glancing around, the battle at the front door had come to a stalemate with the others pouring enough fire towards the beasts outside to keep them from getting inside, at least for the moment.

Racing into the room, Brook was taken aback by what she saw. One of the Sasquatch had literally rammed through the exterior wall of the house. There was a hole in its wake that made her think of the old Kool-aid Man ads. Pieces of busted up wood lay on the floor. The beast must have immediately noticed Larson where she was tied to the chair and went at her. The massive thing was knelt before Larson. Her abdomen was open, the beast's hands going in and out of it, shoveling bloody bits of her organs into its mouth. Larson's eyes were open wide but devoid of life, her head tilted sideways in death, as if watching the beast that was making a meal of her. The gory sight was too much for Brook somehow and she screamed, hating herself for it. The Sasquatch's head snapped around in her direction, burning red eyes fixing onto her. Its lips and the hair around them were smeared with Larson's blood and a chunk of something that might have been her liver was sticking out of its mouth.

Jerking up the barrel of her AR-15 towards the monster, Brook let loose on it. The AR-15 barked again and again as she unloaded nearly half the rifle's magazine into the beast. Bullets pounded its upper body, slamming into the thick muscles of its shoulders with no real effect. The ones that struck the beast's face and head though certainly got a response out of it. The beast stood straight up in its rage, unintentionally smashing its head into the ceiling. That screw up bought Brook the time she needed to finish emptying her weapon into the thing. The Sasquatch shook and twisted as the bullets drew blood. The Sasquatch's body was covered with dozens of wounds but none of them were severe enough to have really hurt it. The shock of its head breaking the boards of the ceiling had done a much better job of hurting the beast.

Brook didn't bother to try to switch out magazines in her AR. Instead, she flung it aside and drew her sidearm. It was a Colt Python and packed a hell of a lot more punch than the AR. As the beast shook its head and righted itself, Brook fired. The high powered round hit the beast in its chin. Bone crumpled beneath the impact of the bullet and blood splashed outward from the wreck of its mouth. The beast tried to roar but the sound that came out was more akin to a muffled, pained shriek. Still, the beast kept coming, staggering across the room towards Brook. Aiming her shot more carefully, Brook fired again, putting a round into the center of the beast's forehead. The bullet crunched the bone of the beast's forehead and entered its brain. Eyes rolling up, the beast fell over, thudding face first onto the floor. Brook wasn't taking any chances. She quickly moved closer to the downed monster and put two more rounds into the backside of its skull. The beast's body spasmed, twitched, and then lay still in a growing pool of its own blood.

The battle at the front of the house continued to rage as Brook left the room, closing it up behind her. The door wouldn't do crap if another of the beasts came through the hole in the wall but it was human impulse to shut it.

Sheriff Levy worked the pump of the shotgun in his hands, chambering a round. Next to him, Jarvis and another of Danny's ex-soldiers held the line against the monsters outside. The girl, Rachel, was passing them ammo and additional weapons as they were needed. So far, they were managing to keep the beasts at bay. It was easy to see that wasn't going to last though. They needed a new plan of action and fast too.

****

Danny had burst out of the bedroom and was sprinting for the stairs. Glancing down over the railing that ran the length of the second floor, he could see the fight downstairs. He needed to join it as quickly as possible. His BMG 50 might just have the power to turn the tide and drive the beasts off. Halfway down the stairs, Danny jumped the railing and landed gracefully on the first floor, holding his rifle tightly so that he didn't lose his grip on it.

"About fragging time you got here!" Jarvis shouted at him.

"Better late than never," Danny quipped, rushing to get into position on the sort of loose firing line the others had formed. Looking out the smashed front doorway, Danny took aim at a Sasquatch charging forward. His BMG 50 boomed. The round it fired nearly blew the beast apart at its waist. Its upper half fell to the left while its lower fell right, tearing loose the strands of sinew that still connected the two. The BMG 50 roared again as Danny shifted his aim and sent another Sasquatch to hell, turning the thing's right shoulder into a bloody, mangled mess.

And just like that. . . the battle was over. The surviving Sasquatch retreated back into the woods, vanishing from sight.

"Damn," Jarvis breathed, a shudder throughout his body. "That was too fragging close."

"They won't stay gone long," Danny pointed out. "You can count on that."

"We need to get the hell out of here while we can," Sheriff Levy snarled.

"Are you insane?" Danny spun on the sheriff.

"Whoa," Jarvis said, moving between them. "Let's try to remember we're all on the same side here, okay?"

"Are we?" Ron cut in.

"What the hell is that supposed to mean?" Danny snarled, glaring at him.

"You know exactly what I mean," Ron said, apparently finally getting enough of a backbone to stand up to Danny. "How many people have died since we came out here? Over half of us, man! No matter what you think, we can't fight these things like this!"

"Look around," Danny snapped, gesturing at the Sasquatch corpses in the house's yard. "We're doing a pretty damn good job of it if you ask me!"

"Sure, we've killed some," Ron admitted, "but that doesn't mean a fragging thing, Danny, and you know it. We've got no idea how many there are. For all we know there's an entire army of them out there."

"Just what are you getting at?" Danny took a step towards Ron but again, Jarvis moved to stop him.

"He's saying the same thing I am, Danny," Sheriff Levy barked. "If we stay here, we're dead. All of us."

"We need to leave," Rachel said quietly but loud enough for everyone to hear her. Her voice was trembling and her eyes wet with tears.

Brook had stayed out of it all until that moment.

Speaking up, Brook said, "I vote we leave too. We're likely not going to get a better chance at it than right now either."

Danny was on the absolute verge of losing it.

"Can't you see?" Danny spat. "Don't you understand? If we go now those things will tear us all apart before we ever make it to the vehicles."

"I don't think so," Ron countered, his words a painful betrayal. "I'm with her and the sheriff. This may be the only chance we're going to get."

"How many rounds you got left for that thing?" Jarvis asked him, motioning at Danny's BMG 50. The question threw him off.

"Four, maybe five," Danny sputtered. "What the hell does that matter?"

Jarvis gave him one of his trademark grins, "It matters because that may be just enough to get us out of here but I damn well wager it's not enough to get the vengeance you're after against all those things. . .sir."

Adding that last word kept Danny from being pushed over the edge and going completely bonkers at how even Jarvis seemed to be turning on him. That word stung and reminded him that he was messing around with more than just his own life. As much as he wanted to see all the beasts out here dead it was likely going to cost a lot more lives to make that happen.

"You know we have to go," Jarvis told him. "I'm sorry, sir, but we do."

Danny's shoulders slumped in defeat. Deep inside of him, he knew Jarvis and the others were right. "Fine."

"Fine?" Jarvis asked, not really believing what he had heard. "What's the catch, man? You planning on not coming with us?"

Danny remembered just how well Jarvis knew him.

"I'm going with you," Danny answered. "I'll help all of you get out of here but I plan on killing every one of those bastard things on the way that I can."

"Fair enough," Jarvis nodded.

"I can live with that too," Sheriff Levy agreed. "Now what say we gather up what we can that we might need and stop wasting time?"

"Get to it then," Danny said, hefting his BMG 50 as if to show it off. "I'll keep watch here."

The others headed back into the house, gathering up weapons, ammo, and gear. Sheriff Levy waited at the front door with him. It felt like the sheriff stayed mainly to keep him from doing anything stupid. Danny couldn't blame the man for that. He'd been far from rational since returning to town. Lost in obsession and then royally screwed in the head when there turned out to be more than one of the beasts, Danny knew he was dangerous. If a man under his command acted like he had, Danny would have had him booted from his squad.

It didn't take long for the others to get ready. The supply of ammo that Danny and his squad had brought along was dwindling quickly. Sheriff Levy's folks had already been using it too. And as to rations, other than some water, there wasn't much point in being anything. The vehicles weren't that far away when you really thought about it and certainly not at the pace they would likely be moving at.

Sheriff Levy took point, leading them into the woods with Danny right behind him. Brook and the girl, Rachel, made up the middle of their loose formation with Ron and Jarvis bringing up the rear. It was still dark enough that they had to move slower than the sheriff seemed to like. They all kept their eyes on the trees surrounding them on all sides. The beasts had proved that they were masters of stealth and weren't to be underestimated. The things could come at them anytime from any direction.

Danny had taken one last look back at the house where the group made its early stand as they left. It had filled him with sadness more than anything.

Not only had he failed in his attempt at vengeance but he'd lost friends there too, friends who had given up their very lives for him. That would weigh on him for the rest of his life no matter how things turned out at this point.

The night was wearing thin as they neared the end of the initial perimeter Danny and his crew had set up. Sheriff Levy didn't see the tripwire obscured by the shadows and underbrush. Its sharp twang rang out as the limb the wire held was freed and sprung forward at him. Sheriff Levy gave a pained grunt as the spike attached to the limb pierced his stomach. Blood rose up his throat and he coughed a mouthful out. It splattered on the limb and the front of his shirt.

"Frag!" Danny yelled, blaming himself. He hadn't realized where the sheriff had been heading in time to warn him off. Danny reached his side and saw that the spike had gotten him good. Its tip protruded from the sheriff's back. Sheriff Levy was still alive. He looked at Danny with desperate eyes that pleaded for help. The others were running up to them but Danny raised a hand, signaling for them to stop where they were. It was better they stayed out of his way.

Danny examined the spike and quickly saw that it wasn't coming out. Pulling it would only worsen the sheriff's wound. . .and the man was dead already. Even if they got the spike out of him, he would bleed out long before they could get him to anywhere that had the ability to properly deal with the severe level of damage that had been done.

Sheriff Levy tried to speak. All that came out was a sickening, gargling noise and more blood that poured over his bottom lip but Danny knew what the sheriff wanted. Holding his BMG 50 with his right hand, Danny drew the .44 Magnum holstered on his hip with his left. Pressing the barrel of the Magnum to the side of Sheriff Levy's skull, he pulled the trigger. The sharp crack of the shot echoed among the trees as the bulk of the sheriff's brains left his skull through the other side of his head. Sheriff Levy's body went limp upon the spike and the limb it was attached to.

Ron and Jarvis ran up to Danny. He returned the heavy pistol to its holster and turned to meet them.

"What the frag did you do that for?" Ron raged.

"It was what he wanted," Danny said plainly, his voice eerily calm.

"That's not what I meant," Ron challenged him. "That shot will draw every one of those things in this area straight to us."

Danny shrugged. "Then I guess we better get moving, huh?"

"Frag you!" Ron snapped and did just that, taking point himself. He pushed on through the trees at a brisk pace, not even looking over his shoulder to see if the others were with him.

"That really sucks," Jarvis commented, staring at Sheriff Levy's corpse.

Brook had moved up to kneel beside the dead man. Her eyes glistened with tears but she didn't let them out. Raising a hand, Brook gently caressed his cheek with her finger tips.

"I'm sorry," Jarvis heard her whisper then Brook got back up.

Jarvis reached out to comfort her but Brook stepped away from him.

"We need to go," Brook told him and followed after Ron.

*And then there were five. . .*Danny thought.

****

Brook could sense the tension between Ron, Danny, and Jarvis. She left it to them and kept her focus on Rachel. Though the girl was armed, an AR-15 in her hands, Rachel didn't have the experience that she or the men had. With the girl being the last real civilian among them, Brook felt obligated to protect her. That was her sworn duty as a deputy, after all. The group's formation had shifted since Sheriff Levy's unexpected demise. It was Danny who brought up the rear now with Ron plowing through the woods on point. She, Jarvis, and Rachel all walked near each other between them.

The early rays of the rising sun cut through the trees, stabbing at the shadows. B rook knew they were getting close to the road where it ended on its way up the mountain and their vehicles were parked. So far, there hadn't been any sign of the Sasquatch coming after them but Brook knew that meant nothing. As skilled at staying silent and unseen as the beasts were, the things could be almost right on top of them and they wouldn't know it.

Danny was the first one out of the woods into the clearing where the vehicles waited, heading straight for the van that belonged to him and his crew. Ron and Jarvis broke to either side as if attempting to secure the area, watching the trees for any sign of the beasts. Brook and Rachel paused just outside of the woods.

And then, the trap was sprung. The beasts had led them right where they wanted them. One of the creatures lurked behind the van and with a thunderous roar shoved the vehicle over at Danny. Startled and caught completely off guard, Danny fired his BMG 50. The high powered round ripped through the van at the Sasquatch on its other side even as the van fell onto him. A muffled scream could be heard from Danny beneath the vehicle just before the Sasquatch leaped up on top of it. The metal of the van crunched and whined under the beast's weight as it leaped again, landing where it faced Ron and Jarvis who were running towards it. Danny had been squished to a red mess and was beyond help though. His blood ran out from beneath the wreckage of the van.

Snapping off a burst of rounds with his M4, Jarvis aimed for the Sasquatch's face and head. The beast brought up its arms with nigh impossible speed, blocking the bulk of the bullets. Ron's shotgun boomed, blowing a chunk of flesh from the beast's left hip. Staggered, the beast reached around to grab the front of a patrol car. The car left the ground as it was swung like a weapon at the two men. Its rear clipped Jarvis, knocking him from his feet and breaking several of his ribs. Ron worked the pump of his shotgun, chambering another round.

"Come on!" Brook yelled at Rachel. She led the girl to the other patrol car.

Flinging its door open, Brook slid into the driver's seat. Fumbling about to get the keys out of her pocket, she saw another Sasquatch entering the clearing. It was much larger than any of the other beasts she had seen. More muscled too. Patches of the hair covering its form were gray indicating that the beast was older than the others. There was a fierce intelligence in its burning, red eyes that scared the hell out of Brook. Finding the keys, she rammed them into the patrol car's ignition. The engine roared to life.

The huge, gray-haired beast advanced on the patrol car. Ron came at the creature from behind its back though, blasting it with his shotgun at near point blank range. Grunting, the monster whirled about on him. A massive, clenched fist swept through the air to make contact with Ron's skull. The former soldier's head exploded like an over ripe melon from the force of the impact.

Jarvis had managed to get to his feet, if just barely. Bracing his M4 against his shoulder, he emptied the weapon into the giant Sasquatch. Brook saw exactly what he was doing. Jarvis was trying to draw the thing away so that she and Rachel could get away. Brook shoved the patrol car into gear, peeling out as she backed up and brought it around to head for the gravel road that led down the mountain.

The other Sasquatch limped towards Jarvis, blood running down its leg from its wounded hip. It stopped though as the larger Sasquatch raised a clawed hand. The action was so human-like that Jarvis could only gawk at the giant Sasquatch in horror. The wounded beast changed its direction and hobbled away into the woods, leaving Jarvis alone with the giant.

Jarvis didn't give a crap, knowing he was about to die. His ploy had worked though. The patrol was gone from sight. All that Jarvis had left to do was buy the girls as much time as he could.

"Come on, you bastard," Jarvis smirked at the giant, tossing his now useless M4 aside. His ribs hurt like hell as he drew the knife sheathed on the side of his boot. He held it ready, holding his ground, waiting for the old beast to come to him. Jarvis would have preferred to have charged the fragging monster and thrown himself onto it but with his ribs like they were, that was impossible.

The giant Sasquatch came stomping its way across the clearing to tower over him. Jarvis lunged forward just as the beast reached him, sinking the blade of his knife into its chest, blade at an upward angle. Ignoring his effort to hurt it, the giant beast closed its hands around his head, lifting Jarvis from the ground by it. Jarvis's legs kicked wildly as the tips of the beast's thumbs sank into his eye sockets. Rivers of red ran down Jarvis's cheeks as he screamed. . .and then his body went limp. The old beast dropped his corpse onto the gravel. It wasn't done with Jarvis though. Raising a massive foot the beast brought it down on Jarvis's head, crushing his skull like a rotten egg.

With the battle over and all those who had intruded into its territory dealt with or fled, the old beast left the clearing and vanished among the trees.

EPILOGUE

Brook had driven straight to the hospital and dropped Rachel off there before heading back to the sheriff department. She said little to the skeleton crew that had been left behind there beyond that Levy and the others were dead.

In the days that followed, Brook became the acting sheriff. When a group was dispatched to the woods in order to retrieve the bodies of those who died, she didn't go with them. Brook swore she was never going in those woods ever again and planned to get the hell out of town as soon as a new sheriff was elected.

No one knew the truth of what happened despite Rachel's attempts to tell the world. Brook made sure that the girl's story was discredited by her own that the group had been attacked by a family of bears. And since none of the bodies were found, no one could dispute Brook's take on things. It was just safer that way, Brook told herself, as if some inner voice warned that if she let out the secret of the beasts that they would come after her and find her no matter where she ran to.

A month later, Brook left for New York without bothering to visit Rachel in the institution where the girl had been locked up. Brook pitied the girl but life was cruel and she had accepted that. Her own future lay in the city, as far from the woods as she could get.

The End

Eric S Brown is the author of numerous book series including the Bigfoot War series, the Psi-Mechs Inc. series, the Kaiju Apocalypse series (with Jason Cordova), the Crypto-Squad series (with Jason Brannon), the Homeworld series (With Tony Faville and Jason Cordova), the Jack Bunny Bam series, and the A Pack of Wolves series. Some of his stand alone books include War of the Worlds plus Blood Guts and Zombies, Casper Alamo (with Jason Brannon), Sasquatch Island, Day of the Sasquatch, Bigfoot, Crashed, World War of the Dead, Last Stand in a Dead Land, Sasquatch Lake, Kaiju Armageddon, Megalodon, Megalodon Apocalypse, Kraken, Alien Battalion, The Last Fleet, and From the Snow They Came to name only a few. His short fiction has been published hundreds of times in the small press in beyond including markets like the Onward Drake and Black Tide Rising anthologies from Baen Books, the Grantville Gazette, the SNAFU Military horror anthology series, and Walmart World magazine. He has done the novelizations for such films as Boggy Creek: The Legend is True (Studio 3 Entertainment) and The Bloody Rage of Bigfoot (Great Lake films). The first book of his Bigfoot War series was adapted into a feature film by Origin Releasing in 2014. Werewolf Massacre at Hell's Gate was the second of his books to be adapted into film in 2015. Major Japanese publisher, Takeshobo, bought the reprint rights to his Kaiju Apocalypse series (with Jason Cordova) and the mass market, Japanese language version was released in late 2017. Ring of Fire Press has released a collected edition of his Monster Society stories (set in the New York Times Best-selling world of Eric Flint's 1632). In addition to his fiction, Eric also writes an award-winning comic book news column entitled "Comics in a Flash" as well a pop culture column for Altered Reality Magazine. Eric lives in North Carolina with his wife and two children where he continues to write tales of the hungry dead, blazing guns, and the things that lurk in the woods.

Check out other great
Cryptid Novels!

Hunter Shea
LOCH NESS REVENGE

Deep in the murky waters of Loch Ness, the creature known as Nessie has returned. Twins Natalie and Austin McQueen watched in horror as their parents were devoured by the world's most infamous lake monster. Two decades later, it's their turn to hunt the legend. But what lurks in the Loch is not what they expected. Nessie is devouring everything in and around the Loch, and it's not alone. Hell has come to the Scottish Highlands. In a fierce battle between man and monster, the world may never be the same. Praise for THEY RISE : "Outrageous, balls to the wall...made me yearn for 3D glasses and a tub of popcorn, extra butter!" – The Eyes of Madness "A fast-paced, gore-heavy splatter fest of sharksploitation." The Werd "A rocket paced horror story. I enjoyed the hell out of this book." Shotgun Logic Reviews

C.G. Mosley
BAKER COUNTY BIGFOOT CHRONICLE

Marie Bledsoe only wants her missing brother Kurt back. She'll stop at nothing to make it happen and, with the help of Kurt's friend Tony, along with Sheriff Ray Cochran, Marie embarks on a terrifying journey deep into the belly of the mysterious Walker Laboratory to find him. However, what she and her companions find lurking in the laboratory basement is beyond comprehension. There are cryptids from the forest being held captive there and something...else. Enjoy this suspenseful tale from the mind of C.G. Mosley, author of Wood Ape. Welcome back to Baker County, a place where monsters do lurk in the night!

Check out other great
Cryptid Novels!

Edward J. McFadden III
THE CRYPTID CLUB

When cryptozoologist Ash Cohn receives a gold embossed printed invitation inviting him to join The Cryptid Club, he sees the resolution to all his problems.Famous cryptid scientist and biologist, Lester Treemont, one of the world's richest men, and the leader of the Cryptid Club, is dying. What he offers via his invitation is a chance to succeed him. To take over his wealth, laboratory, and discoveries. All Ash has to do is beat eight others like him in a series of tests both mental and physical involving Treemont's collection of cryptids. Seems simple enough, and Ash has nothing to lose.Nine strangers from across the globe, all with reasons for wanting to win. When they start dying one by one, the competition shifts to one of survival. Who among them will rise to the top and reign over The Cryptid Club?

William Meikle
INFESTATION

It was supposed to be a simple mission. A suspected Russian spy boat is in trouble in Canadian waters. Investigate and report are the orders. But when Captain John Banks and his squad arrive, it is to find an empty vessel, and a scene of bloody mayhem. Soon they are in a fight for their lives, for there are things in the icy seas off Baffin Island, scuttling, hungry things with a taste for human flesh. They are swarming. And they are growing. "Scotland's best Horror writer" - Ginger Nuts of Horror "The premier storyteller of our time." - Famous Monsters of Filmland

Check out other great
Cryptid Novels!

Hunter Shea
THE DOVER DEMON

The Dover Demon is real...and it has returned. In 1977, Sam Brogna and his friends came upon a terrifying, alien creature on a deserted country road. What they witnessed was so bizarre, so chilling, they swore their silence. But their lives were changed forever. Decades later, the town of Dover has been hit by a massive blizzard. Sam's son, Nicky, is drawn to search for the infamous cryptid, only to disappear into the bowels of a secret underground lair. The Dover Demon is far deadlier than anyone could have believed. And there are many of them. Can Sam and his reunited friends rescue Nicky and battle a race of creatures so powerful, so sinister, that history itself has been shaped by their secretive presence? "THE DOVER DEMON is Shea's most delightful and insidiously terrifying monster yet." – Shotgun Logic Reviews "An excellent horror novel and a strong standout in the UFO and cryptid subgenres." –Hellnotes "Non-stop action awaits those brave enough to dive into the small town of Dover, and if you're lucky, you won't see the Demon himself!" – The Scary Reviews PRAISE FOR SWAMP MONSTER MASSACRE "B-horror movie fans rejoice, Hunter Shea is here to bring you the ultimate tale of terror!" – Horror Novel Reviews "A nonstop thrill ride! I couldn't put this book down." – Cedar Hollow Horror Reviews

Armand Rosamilia
THE BEAST

The end of summer, 1986. With only a few days left until the new school year, twins Jeremy and Jack Schaffer are on very different paths. Jeremy is the geek, playing Dungeons & Dragons with friends Kathleen and Randy, while Jack is the jock, getting into trouble with his buddies. And then everything changes when neighbor Mister Higgins is killed by a wild animal in his yard. Was it a bear? There's something big lurking in the woods behind their New Jersey home. Will the police be able to solve the murder before more Middletown residents are ripped apart?